Breaking Barriers

La'Shayla Godfrey

www.theinkwellpublishingcompany.com

ISBN: 979-8-89502-011-1 (hardback) | 979-8-89502012-8 (paperback) | 979-8-89502-013-5 (ebook)

Publication Data
Subjects: Emotional Healing; Friendship; Identity; Forgiveness
Keyword: What it means to rebuild trust when everything's broken
Short Description: A vulnerable, heartfelt coming-of-age story for anyone who's ever had to lose someone to find themselves. "Breaking Barriers" reminds us that love isn't just about romance—it's about truth, forgiveness, and choosing each other again.

This is a work of fiction inspired by the author's imagination and experiences. While elements of the story may draw from reality, any resemblance to actual persons, organizations, or events—beyond those intentionally referenced—is entirely coincidental.

Printed in the United States of America
1st Printing
Editor: Demetri D. Long
Cover Designer & Illustrator: La'Shayla Godfrey
Formator: Demetri D. Long

For Demetri,

My best friend, my steady place.
Through every shift, every high and low, you've been there—
not perfectly, not always

smoothly, but always real. Ours isn't the kind of friendship that
needs to be loud to be
strong. It's quiet resilience. It's knowing when to give space and
when to show up. It's the
unspoken understanding that no matter how far apart we drift
or how tense things get,
we'll always find our way back.

You've been the person I can be my truest self with, even when
that self is messy or
uncertain. Thank you for seeing me, for staying, and for
teaching me what it means to grow
with someone instead of apart.

This story is about breaking barriers. You and I have broken a
few of our own—but we've
built something better in their place. This one's for you.

Chapter 1
Friction and First Impressions

Leila's sophomore year at Westbrook High took an unexpected turn the day she was paired with Destiny Carter for their history project. With her laid-back attitude and tendency to procrastinate, Leila was the polar opposite of Destiny—meticulous, driven, and fiercely independent. Their first meeting after school was a disaster. Leila showed up late and disorganized, her notes scribbled on the back of a math worksheet, while Destiny sat waiting with neatly arranged outlines and color-coded tabs. It didn't take long for frustration to flare. Destiny's sharp remarks about Leila's lack of preparedness stung, and Leila, annoyed by Destiny's perfectionist streak, rolled her eyes and blew it off.

The following day, Destiny refused to make eye contact, her answers clipped and formal. Despite the tension, Leila's guilt nagged at her. She sent a brief apology text that night, and though Destiny's response was brief—just a curt, "Don't do it again"—it was enough to keep the project afloat. Their next study session at the library was awkward at first, filled with stiff silences and mechanical collaboration. But gradually, the tension eased. Leila's dry humor slipped through Destiny's icy exterior, earning an unexpected smirk. Over time, the hours spent combing through textbooks and swapping notes became more bearable. Destiny's wit, once masked by her reserved demeanor, surfaced with teasing remarks, and Leila found herself eagerly sparring back. They began to linger a little longer after finishing their work, talking about classes, teachers, and eventually their own lives. Leila shared stories about her chaotic home with two younger siblings, while Destiny spoke reluctantly about the pressures of living up to her older sister's academic legacy. Their guarded walls slowly came down.

One rainy afternoon, they huddled by the window in the library, laughing over a shared playlist. When Destiny shyly offered one of her earbuds to Leila, their fingers brushed—just for a second—but the warmth lingered. Leila realized she was noticing the tiny dimple in Destiny's left cheek whenever she smiled and the way her eyes softened when she was lost in thought. It caught Leila off guard—the way Destiny's presence had become comfortable, and familiar, and how much she now craved it. Neither of them acknowledged the shift aloud, but it was there, woven into the easy silences and the glances they held for a second too long. What started as a reluctant partnership had unexpectedly transformed into something that neither of them could walk away from, even if they weren't yet ready to name it.

Leila flopped onto her bed with a groan, tossing her backpack onto the floor. Her room was a mess—crumpled hoodies, mismatched socks, and textbooks scattered across the floor. She stared at the ceiling for a moment, replaying the day in her mind. The school day had dragged on, but the only part she kept coming back to was the time she'd spent with Destiny. It had become the best part of her day, and she wasn't sure when that had started.

Her phone buzzed on the nightstand. She rolled over and grabbed it, her stomach tightening slightly when she saw Destiny's name pop up.

Destiny: *You're late on the notes for Chapter 7. Again.* 🙄

Leila: *I work better under pressure. It's called the thrill of the deadline.* 😎

Destiny: *It's called being irresponsible.*

Leila: *Whoa. Do I detect a hint of fondness behind that* *judgment?*

Destiny: *In your dreams.*

Leila grinned at her screen. Lately, their conversations had become more than just about their history project. The teasing, the snarky banter—it made her heart beat a little faster. It was becoming effortless, natural, in a way that made Leila both excited and uneasy. She opened their chat again and hesitated before typing.

Leila: *Hey, you wanna meet at the library tomorrow? Or we can ditch and grab milkshakes instead. I hear rebellion is good for the soul.* 😎

She stared at the message, her thumb hovering over the **send** button. She wasn't sure why she was so nervous—it was just a study date. Right? But before she could overthink it, she hit send and quickly locked her phone, tossing it on the bed as if that would make the anxiety go away.

The screen stayed dark for several agonizing minutes. Leila grabbed a pillow and smacked it against her face, muffling a groan. She was being ridiculous. Then, her phone buzzed. She snatched it up faster than she wanted to admit.

Destiny: *Milkshakes, huh? That's a bold move for a slacker.*

Destiny: *But fine. One hour. Don't be late.*

Leila flopped back onto her bed with a wide grin.

The next day, the air was warm and sticky—the late September humidity still clinging stubbornly despite the leaves turning amber and rust. Leila waited outside **Penny's Diner**, fidgeting with her phone. She wiped her palms against her jeans, glancing at the cracked screen to check the time. She was five minutes early—a rare accomplishment.

When she spotted Destiny walking toward her, Leila straightened up without thinking. Destiny wore a loose, faded denim jacket over a fitted black tank top, paired with her usual skinny jeans. Her hair was pulled into a low ponytail, but a few loose strands had slipped free, framing her face. Leila's breath caught unexpectedly.

"Wow, you're on time," Destiny teased as she walked up. "Miracles do happen."

Leila smirked. "I like to keep you on your toes. Gotta maintain the mystery."

Destiny rolled her eyes, but Leila caught the smile tugging at the corners of her lips.

They grabbed a booth near the window. The diner was small and old-fashioned, with red vinyl seats and checkered tile floors. The bell over the door jingled every time someone walked in, but the diner was mostly quiet, filled with only the occasional murmur of conversation.

They ordered their milkshakes—strawberry for Destiny, chocolate for Leila—and settled into the booth. For the first few minutes, they kept the conversation light, chatting about teachers and the ridiculous amount of homework they had. But eventually, the easy banter gave way to something quieter.

Leila stirred her milkshake with her straw, watching the way the melted ice cream spiraled in her glass. "You ever just wanna... disappear for a while?" she asked suddenly.

Destiny looked at her, frowning slightly. "Like run away?"

Leila shrugged, her gaze still down. "Not forever. Just... long enough to breathe."

There was a pause. Leila didn't expect Destiny to understand. She seemed so put-together—so controlled. But then Destiny quietly said, "Yeah. All the time."

Leila glanced up, surprised by the admission. She searched Destiny's expression, but her eyes were focused on the condensation on her glass, fingers tracing shapes absently.

"Why?" Leila asked softly.

Destiny let out a breath, leaning back against the booth. She glanced out the window, her eyes distant. "Sometimes it feels like everyone already knows what I'm supposed to be. Like I'm on this... conveyor belt. Honor roll. AP classes. Student council. The 'perfect daughter.'" She exhaled sharply and shook her head. "It's just... a lot."

Leila's chest tightened unexpectedly. She wasn't used to seeing Destiny as anything but composed. Vulnerable Destiny caught her off guard.

"Hey," Leila said, reaching across the table before she could second-guess herself. She hesitated briefly, then let her fingers graze Destiny's wrist. "You don't have to be perfect all the time, you know."

Destiny's eyes flicked down to where Leila's hand rested on her skin. For a brief moment, she didn't move. Her gaze lingered, her lips parting slightly as if she wanted to say something but couldn't quite find the words.

Then she slowly flipped her hand over, her palm brushing against Leila's. She didn't pull away.

Leila's pulse quickened, but she didn't let go. They sat there for a long moment, fingers barely touching, neither of them saying a word. It was nothing. And everything.

The bell over the door jingled, and Destiny abruptly pulled her hand back. She cleared her throat, suddenly looking anywhere but at Leila.

"Sorry," Destiny mumbled, grabbing her milkshake and taking a long sip.

Leila quickly pulled her hand back, her heart thudding unevenly. "No, it's—it's fine," she said quickly, forcing a laugh she didn't feel. "Just a sugar rush or something."

Destiny didn't meet her eyes.

They left the diner a few minutes later, the awkwardness hanging between them like thick fog. Leila shoved her hands into her jacket pockets, unsure of what to say. She felt stupid for misreading the moment. Maybe it had just been in her head.

But when they reached the end of the block, Destiny slowed. She turned slightly, her eyes still downcast.

"Hey," she said quietly. "Thanks... for tonight."

Leila glanced at her, searching her face for a sign of what she was feeling. But Destiny's expression was carefully guarded again, her mask back in place.

"Anytime," Leila said softly, her voice barely above a whisper.

Destiny gave her a small smile, the kind that didn't quite reach her eyes. She turned and walked away, her silhouette blending into the dim light.

Leila stood there for a moment, watching her disappear into the night. She exhaled sharply and ran a hand through her hair, her fingers shaking slightly.

Her phone buzzed in her pocket. She pulled it out, already knowing who it was before she saw the name.

Destiny: *See you tomorrow?*

Leila stared at the message, her heart doing a strange, fluttering flip in her chest. She smiled faintly, her fingers hovering over the keyboard before she typed back.

Leila: *Yeah. Definitely.*

She shoved her phone back into her pocket, but the warmth stayed with her all the way home.

The next morning, Leila woke up earlier than usual. Her alarm hadn't even gone off yet, and she was already wide awake, her mind buzzing with thoughts of the night before. It was strange. It felt like she was walking on the edge of something she couldn't quite define. Her fingers ached from the ghost of Destiny's touch, and the memory of the way their hands had almost connected lingered, unspoken but undeniable.

She threw off her blanket and stumbled toward the bathroom, splashing cold water on her face to shake off the grogginess. Her reflection stared back at her in the mirror, bleary-eyed but more awake than usual. There was a new flutter in her chest that she couldn't ignore, something that didn't quite feel like nerves but wasn't quite excitement either. Maybe it was anticipation.

By the time she got dressed and grabbed her things for school, her phone buzzed again. The message was from Destiny.

Destiny: *You awake?*

Leila couldn't help the small smile that tugged at her lips as she typed back.

Leila: *Just about to leave. You?*

Destiny: *Already waiting for you at the bus stop. Hurry up, slacker.*

Leila chuckled. She quickly grabbed her backpack and ran out the door, the cool morning air hitting her like a refreshing splash of water. The sun was still low, casting long shadows over the street, but it was already warm.

When she reached the bus stop, Destiny was standing by the curb, fiddling with her phone, as usual. She didn't look up when

Leila approached, and for a moment, Leila just watched her—watched the way she moved, the way she seemed so effortlessly put together despite the fact that it was early and neither of them had gotten much sleep. There was something mesmerizing about it.

"Hey," Leila said, grinning as she stepped up next to her.

Destiny looked up, offering a small smile, the corners of her mouth lifting slightly, but she said nothing. She just shoved her phone back into her pocket and stood there, waiting.

Leila felt a flush creep up her neck but didn't look away. "What's up?" she asked casually, trying to keep her voice steady as if it didn't feel like her heart was beating too loudly.

"I was just thinking about the project," Destiny said, her voice soft. "We need to figure out how we're going to divide the work. I don't want to end up doing everything again."

Leila raised an eyebrow, stifling a grin. "Me? Do everything? You must have me confused with someone else."

Destiny gave her a skeptical look. "I've seen your notes. We both know how this goes."

Leila laughed, nudging her playfully with her shoulder. "Okay, okay. I'll step up my game this time. Promise."

Destiny didn't answer, but the way she tilted her head, a slight hint of amusement in her eyes, made Leila feel like maybe, just maybe, they were starting to find a rhythm together.

The bus arrived a few minutes later, and they climbed on together, heading toward their usual seats in the back. Leila tried not to notice how easily their shoulders brushed when they sat down side by side, how every movement felt charged with something new.

The rest of the ride to school passed in a blur of half-hearted conversation about the project, some idle gossip about teachers, and the usual jokes about the absurdity of high school life. But Leila could feel the shift in the air between them, the way it was different now—more comfortable, less awkward. It wasn't just about school anymore. She felt it in the way Destiny's gaze lingered a little longer, the way their words had started to carry more weight than they ever had before.

When they got to school, Destiny's smile was a little warmer, a little less guarded than usual. Leila couldn't stop herself from smiling back, feeling like she'd unlocked something in Destiny, something she'd never seen before.

They parted ways at the entrance, heading to their respective classes. But as Leila walked to her locker, she couldn't help but think about how easy it had been with Destiny. How, despite the history between them, despite everything that had happened, it felt like maybe—just maybe—they could start over.

By the time the final bell rang, signaling the end of the school day, Leila was eager to see Destiny again. They had agreed to meet up in the library after school to work on the project, but Leila was already thinking about the conversation they'd had that morning, about the way Destiny had looked at her when she talked about the project.

Leila hadn't realized just how much she wanted to impress Destiny until now. She wanted to be someone who mattered, someone who could match her wit and intelligence, someone who could keep up. But more than that, she wanted Destiny to see her in a way that she hadn't before. She wanted to be seen as more than just the girl who always managed to be the class clown, always skimming by with just enough effort.

When she entered the library, Destiny was already there, sitting at one of the tables, her books spread out in front of her. She didn't notice Leila walk in, her focus entirely on the pages in front of her. Leila stood for a moment, watching her, wondering what was going on in her mind.

"Hey," Leila said, walking up to the table.

Destiny looked up, her expression softening into something between relief and fondness. "You're on time for once."

Leila grinned. "I told you I work better under pressure."

Destiny snorted, but it was the kind of laugh that seemed to come easily now, the kind that didn't need to be forced.

As they sat down and began working on the project, the conversation drifted naturally. They were no longer just two people who had been forced together by a school assignment. Something had changed, something that neither of them could quite explain. It wasn't just the project anymore. It was about what they were building, the foundation they were laying without even realizing it.

And, as Leila glanced over at Destiny, watching the way the sunlight filtered through the library's windows and illuminated her features, she realized that maybe, just maybe, this was the start of something real. Something that could last beyond the halls of high school.

Leila couldn't help but notice the way Destiny's eyes narrowed in concentration as she scribbled down notes, her brow furrowed. There was something different about her today—something more relaxed, less guarded. Maybe it was just the project, the quiet time they were sharing, or maybe it was the fact that they were finally getting along for the first time in a while. Either way, it felt like progress. Real progress.

The library was mostly empty, the soft hum of the fluorescent lights filling the air as they worked in silence. Leila's focus shifted between the notes on her laptop and the occasional glance at Destiny, who seemed so immersed in the task at hand. She had always admired how driven Destiny was—how she could dive into anything with such dedication. But today, something felt... different. There was a shift. It wasn't just about school anymore. It was about something more tangible, more real.

"So," Leila said, breaking the silence, "how's the project looking from your end?"

Destiny didn't immediately respond, but she paused, her pen hovering above the paper as she gave Leila a quick glance. "Honestly? I think it's coming together pretty well. I was thinking we could split the presentation into two parts—each of us handling one section."

Leila nodded thoughtfully. "That sounds fair. I'll take the research side. You always do better with the visuals anyway."

Destiny smiled faintly. "You're not wrong."

Leila smiled back, but it wasn't just a typical grin. There was something about the way Destiny's smile reached her eyes that made Leila feel like they were on the same wavelength now. It wasn't forced, and it wasn't awkward. It was just... comfortable.

As they continued to work, the hours seemed to fly by. The occasional chatter and laughs punctuated their efforts, and the more they worked, the more Leila realized that this wasn't just a project anymore. This was a chance for something deeper to form between them. They had spent years tiptoeing around each other, exchanging barbs and getting under each other's skin. But here they were, working side by side as partners, like it had always been meant to be this way.

"Okay, so let's go over this again," Destiny said after some time, pushing the papers in front of Leila as she leaned in. "We've got our research, and we're pretty solid on that. Now we just need to finalize our visual aids, make sure everything flows, and—"

"Make sure it doesn't suck?" Leila interrupted with a playful grin.

Destiny laughed, the sound genuine and light. It felt like a small victory. Leila hadn't heard that laugh in a while—at least not around her. It was always guarded, always a little strained. But now, it was easy. Natural. She liked it.

"Exactly," Destiny said, her voice laced with mock seriousness. "This is important, Leila. We can't afford to look stupid in front of the whole class."

Leila raised her hands in mock surrender. "Hey, I'm just here to make you look good. You're the one who knows how to present."

Destiny glanced up at her, eyes narrowing in feigned suspicion. "Is that so? I seem to remember you being pretty good at handling things when you put your mind to it."

Leila's cheeks flushed at the unexpected compliment. She wasn't used to hearing things like that from Destiny. Sure, they had always been frenemies, always sharp with each other, but there was a different tone in Destiny's voice now. It wasn't just playful teasing. There was an undercurrent of respect.

The conversation flowed easily after that, and before Leila knew it, the library was closing. They hadn't even realized how much time had passed, completely absorbed in their work. As they packed up their things, Leila felt a strange sense of reluctance. She hadn't wanted the day to end. There was something about spending time with Destiny in this quiet, focused environment that made everything feel simpler and clearer.

"So," Leila said as they made their way toward the library doors, "I guess we're done for today. You want to walk home with me?" She offered a casual shrug, but she couldn't hide the hopeful edge in her voice.

Destiny paused, looking down at her phone for a moment before slipping it into her pocket. "Sure, why not?" she replied, her tone light. "It'll give us more time to talk about... whatever. The project or whatever else."

Leila smiled, feeling a little thrill at the fact that they had just made plans to hang out outside of school. This wasn't just about the project anymore. Something had shifted. Something had changed, and it felt right.

They walked out of the library side by side, the cool evening air brushing against their skin as they made their way down the street. It was a quiet walk, the hum of the city around them, the distant chatter of students heading home, but there was an ease to the silence. They didn't need to fill it with words. It was enough just being in each other's company, sharing the same space for the first time without the usual tension between them.

"So, what are you going to do after this project is over?" Leila asked after a while, glancing over at Destiny, who was lost in thought.

Destiny shrugged. "Probably go home and chill for a bit. You know, the usual. Watch Netflix. Get some food. You?"

"Same," Leila said with a chuckle. "Maybe I'll actually do something productive for once, but no promises."

Destiny shot her a sideways glance, her lips twitching as if she might smile but was holding it back. "Good luck with that," she teased.

Leila laughed, the sound light and free. "I'm serious this time! I've got goals."

"Sure, sure," Destiny said, her tone dripping with mock sarcasm. "I'll believe it when I see it."

Leila rolled her eyes, but there was no real bite to her response. "Okay, but seriously. I don't know. I'm thinking about... I don't know, maybe focusing more on my grades this semester. Maybe even getting a head start on some stuff for next year."

"Wow," Destiny said, raising an eyebrow. "Look at you, planning ahead. I'm impressed."

Leila grinned, shrugging. "Hey, sometimes I have my moments."

They were almost to Leila's house when Destiny stopped walking, turning to face her with a serious expression. "Hey," she said quietly, "I just wanted to say... thanks. For today. I know we've had our issues, but... I don't know, this was good. It was nice to actually work together without all the drama."

Leila's heart skipped a beat. She hadn't been expecting that. She had expected something lighter, a joke, a tease, but not this.

"No problem," Leila said softly, her voice earnest. "I... I think I'm glad we're doing this. Really."

For a moment, they just stood there, staring at each other, neither of them knowing quite what to say next. But for once, there was no tension between them. No resentment. Just two people, standing on the edge of something new, something better.

Leila's house came into view as they walked down the quiet suburban street. The golden glow of the streetlights cast long shadows on the sidewalk, and the evening air had a crisp bite to it. For a moment, the thought of going back inside her house seemed like a small disappointment—she had gotten used to the ease between herself and Destiny. It had been years since they had talked without feeling the weight of all their past issues hovering in the air like a constant reminder of everything that hadn't worked between them.

"I guess this is me," Leila said, glancing at her house, which stood a few steps ahead. She slowed her pace, not wanting the moment to end just yet.

Destiny stopped beside her, her hands stuffed in the pockets of her jacket, but there was no urgency to leave. For a brief moment, they simply stood there. The usual awkwardness they had once shared seemed to have dissolved.

"So," Leila started, her voice a little softer than usual, "same time tomorrow to work on the project? I feel like we're almost there, but we still need to fine-tune things."

"Yeah," Destiny replied after a beat, her gaze still fixed ahead. "Same time. I think we've got a pretty good shot at making this work."

A part of Leila wanted to ask if she really meant that—if they really meant that—but she didn't. She wasn't sure if they were on the verge of something more than just a successful project. For years, she had imagined this moment with Destiny as a distant dream, a fleeting possibility. They had been too different, too tangled up in the history of their rivalry, to really be friends. But now, standing on the cusp of their newfound camaraderie, it felt like they were finally breaking free of their old patterns.

"Cool," Leila said, forcing herself to sound casual. "See you tomorrow."

"See you," Destiny replied, before turning to walk down the sidewalk in the opposite direction. Leila watched her go, her hands still in her pockets as she tried to ignore the small smile tugging at her lips. It wasn't much, but it was enough. Enough to make her believe that maybe, just maybe, this time things could be different.

The next few days passed in a blur of late-night study sessions, project preparations, and surprisingly comfortable conversations between Leila and Destiny. Every day seemed to bring a new discovery about each other, a new shared interest, or a small personal revelation that added depth to their friendship.

One afternoon, as they worked together in the library again, Destiny leaned over her laptop, furrowing her brow as she scanned the data they had compiled for their project. Leila sat across from her, idly flipping through some notes while glancing at her phone.

"You're looking stressed," Leila remarked, noting the furrow in Destiny's brow. "What's up?"

Destiny let out a long sigh, pushing her hair back from her face. "It's nothing major," she said, her voice uncharacteristically quiet. "I just... I don't know. There's a lot going on right now. School's kind of overwhelming, and I'm worried about my grades in some classes."

Leila raised an eyebrow, a little surprised by the admission. Destiny wasn't exactly the type to openly admit she was struggling. In fact, most people probably wouldn't guess that she had anything less than perfect control over her life. Leila herself had always been a bit envious of Destiny's confidence, her seemingly effortless success. But now, hearing her speak like this, she realized that maybe Destiny wasn't as invincible as she appeared.

"Hey," Leila said, setting her phone down on the table and meeting Destiny's eyes. "If you need help with anything, just ask. You know, I'm here. We're partners, right?"

Destiny hesitated, her eyes flicking between Leila's face and the screen of her laptop. For a brief moment, it seemed like she was wrestling with herself as if asking for help was a foreign concept to her.

"I don't want to be a burden," Destiny finally said, her voice low.

Leila shook her head, leaning forward. "You're not a burden. Honestly. I know we've had our issues in the past, but that's... that's behind us, okay? I actually like working with you. It feels good, and I mean that. So if there's something you need help with, just ask."

For a long beat, Destiny didn't say anything. She simply stared at Leila, her expression unreadable. Leila could see the wheels turning in her mind, the hesitation, the internal conflict.

Finally, Destiny nodded, her shoulders relaxing slightly. "Thanks, Leila. I guess... I guess I could use some help with the history project for U.S. History. I'm kind of falling behind on the research part."

"Done," Leila said with a smile. "We'll tackle that next session."

As they fell into their routine of working together, something in Leila shifted. She had spent years watching Destiny from a distance, judging her from the sidelines. She had been quick to categorize her as just another competitor in a long line of people she had to outshine. But now, as they spent more time together, she saw the cracks in that exterior, the parts of Destiny that no one else saw—the vulnerability, the self-doubt, the parts that made her human. It made Leila realize how much she had misjudged her.

Over the next few days, their project continued to come together, each of them contributing in ways that complemented the other. Leila found herself learning more from Destiny than she had expected. Her insights, her approach to solving problems, even her sense of humor—it all fascinated Leila. She hadn't expected that. She hadn't expected to respect her in this way, but she did.

And as they worked, something else started to grow between them—something deeper, something that had always been buried under the weight of their rivalry. The more they shared, the more they realized how much they had in common. It wasn't just about school anymore. It was about connecting on a human level, about shedding the layers of judgment and misunderstanding they had built up over the years.

One evening, after another productive study session, they decided to take a break. The conversation shifted from school to more personal matters—what they wanted to do after graduation, their favorite music, and even their embarrassing childhood stories.

"So, I'll admit it," Destiny said, a playful glint in her eyes. "I used to think you were just another stuck-up overachiever."

Leila blinked in surprise, laughing at the unexpected comment. "Me? Stuck-up? You've got to be kidding."

"Yeah, I know, right?" Destiny chuckled. "But I thought you were always so perfect. Like, you had it all figured out."

Leila leaned back in her chair, thinking for a moment. "You know what? I kind of thought the same thing about you. Like, you were just... the cool, confident girl who had everything handed to her."

Destiny snorted. "I wish. Believe me, there's a lot more going on behind the scenes than you think."

Leila smiled, feeling a warmth spread through her chest. This—this was what she had been missing all these years. The real connection. The true friendship.

"Well," she said, "I'm glad we got over that whole 'hating each other' thing."

Destiny grinned, her eyes lighting up. "Yeah. Me too."

And for the first time, Leila realized that they were no longer just working together on a school project. They were building something much more important—a real friendship, one that was finally being built on honesty, understanding, and mutual respect.

The sun had long since dipped below the horizon by the time Leila entered her house, the cool air of the evening still clinging to her jacket as she closed the door behind her. Her mind was buzzing with thoughts of the day—their unexpected success in the project, the way Destiny had finally opened up, and the way things between them felt different. It wasn't just the project anymore. Something deeper was at play, and Leila wasn't sure if she was ready for it.

She hung up her jacket on the back of the door and tossed her backpack onto the couch, then collapsed onto the cushions with a sigh. The evening had left her exhausted but oddly content. There was a strange weightlessness in her chest as if she had just crossed some invisible threshold into a new phase of her relationship with Destiny. But what was it? She couldn't quite name it yet, but she didn't need to. For now, it was enough to just let the feeling linger.

Her phone buzzed from the coffee table, and she grabbed it without thinking. It was a text from Destiny.

Thanks for today. It actually felt like we got somewhere. Hope we can keep this up.

Leila smiled at the message. She hadn't realized how much she needed to hear that. Even in all their years of being rivals, this was the first time Destiny had truly acknowledged their shared effort. And to hear her say it felt like progress—it felt like something real.

Definitely. I'm glad we did this. Same time tomorrow?

She hit send and then dropped the phone back onto the table, not waiting for a response. She was already thinking ahead— about the project, about school, and about Destiny. And yet, beneath the thoughts that filled her head, there was another, quieter realization: her relationship with Destiny had never felt like this before. For the first time in a long while, it didn't feel like they were battling for the top spot. It felt like they were... partners.

She sat up, rubbing her eyes. The day had left her with more questions than answers, but the answers didn't seem urgent. They could wait. What mattered was that, for the first time, she had felt seen—not just as a student, not just as someone who needed to be perfect, but as someone who was truly connecting with another person. And that connection, that small spark of understanding, was something she hadn't realized she'd been missing all along.

The next morning came too soon. Leila dragged herself out of bed and quickly got ready for the day. The weight of her thoughts from the night before hung on her like a low hum, a feeling she couldn't shake no matter how much she tried to focus on her morning routine. Her usual automatic movements seemed slower today, as though her body couldn't quite keep up with her mind.

She walked to school with a familiar sense of anticipation, but it wasn't the same as it used to be. She wasn't worried about getting through the day or trying to one-up her classmates. No, now, her thoughts kept returning to the project—what they had accomplished yesterday, what they could accomplish today—and, more than that, to Destiny. She couldn't stop thinking about the quiet vulnerability she had glimpsed in her when she had admitted her struggles the day before.

When Leila arrived at school, she made her way straight to the library to meet Destiny, arriving early as usual. She didn't know why she was so eager to get to the project; it wasn't like her. But there was something about how their work together felt... different. It was almost as if their collaboration had moved beyond just a school assignment. It had become something deeper, something that spoke to a connection that neither of them had fully explored before.

Destiny was already there, sitting at their usual table, her laptop open and her eyes focused on the screen. She didn't look up as Leila approached, but there was a subtle shift in her posture—something that suggested she had noticed her presence before Leila had even spoken.

"Morning," Leila greeted, slipping into the seat across from her.

"Morning," Destiny replied, her eyes briefly flickering up to meet Leila's before she returned to her laptop screen. "Ready to dive back in?"

Leila gave a half-smile, feeling the familiar spark of competition between them but not the usual tension. It was still there, of course. They were both driven, both striving for the best, but today, it didn't feel like an obstacle. It felt more like the fuel that would make their partnership work.

"Yeah, let's get to it," Leila said, rolling up her sleeves and opening her own laptop.

The next few hours passed in a whirlwind of research, discussion, and ideas. There was no room for negativity or competitiveness, just a steady flow of collaboration. Destiny and Leila worked seamlessly, bouncing ideas off each other and refining their work in ways neither had anticipated. They were both deeply invested in the project, but it wasn't just the work they cared about anymore. It was the process—the way they had learned to respect each other's strengths, the way they had both lowered their defenses and allowed the other in.

As the clock ticked down to their final hour together, Leila found herself realizing something. The project was nearly finished, but they weren't done. Not yet.

"So," Leila began, pushing her hair out of her face as she leaned back in her chair, "we've made a lot of progress, huh?"

"Yeah, we're almost there," Destiny agreed, her fingers still moving quickly across the keyboard. "I think we just need to add a few finishing touches and we're golden."

Leila smiled, but this time, it wasn't just about the project. It was about something else. She looked at Destiny and saw not just the girl she had once called an enemy, but someone who had, against all odds, become a real friend.

"You know, I didn't think this would work out," Leila said, the words slipping out before she could stop them. "I thought we'd just get the project done and then go our separate ways."

Destiny raised an eyebrow, her fingers pausing mid-type. "Yeah?"

"Yeah," Leila admitted, laughing a little at herself. "But honestly, I'm glad we're doing this together. It feels... good."

There was a beat of silence before Destiny's lips twitched into a smile, and for a moment, she actually seemed at ease. "Me too," she said softly, her voice carrying a sincerity that made Leila's heart skip a beat.

Leila wasn't sure when it had happened—when the shift had occurred. She couldn't pinpoint the exact moment when they had gone from being classmates to rivals to something much more significant. But as she sat there with Destiny, feeling the weight of their mutual understanding, she realized that this was how it was supposed to be. Not just for the project, but for their lives moving forward.

They didn't have all the answers yet, but they were figuring it out together.

The bell rang, signaling the end of their time in the library, and Destiny quickly saved their work, her fingers moving with practiced ease.

"I guess that's it for today," Destiny said, looking up at Leila with a glance that felt almost... warm.

"Guess so," Leila replied, standing up and gathering her things. "Same time tomorrow?"

"Same time," Destiny said with a nod.

Leila walked out of the library, a sense of quiet contentment settling over her. She hadn't realized how much she needed this, how much she needed Destiny, until now. The project was almost finished, but for the first time in a long time, it wasn't the end of something—it was just the beginning.

Chapter 2
New Beginnings

Leila couldn't shake off the feeling that she had just made the wrong impression. The entire walk home, she replayed the events in her head, each moment feeling more awkward than the last. Destiny's smug smile, the way her voice had hardened when they spoke—it all left Leila feeling exposed, like she was the one who'd lost. She tried to tell herself it was just one of those things that happened in high school, that Destiny wasn't worth her time. But deep down, she knew that wasn't true.

The next day at school, Leila's head was heavy with the anxiety of seeing Destiny again. When she entered the classroom, she scanned the room for her, but Destiny wasn't sitting at her usual desk. In fact, there was no sign of her at all. Leila's chest tightened as she slid into her own seat, trying to push the uncomfortable thoughts from her mind.

"Hey, you're early today," Maya, her best friend, said, sliding into the seat beside her. Leila forced a smile, but it didn't reach her eyes.

"Yeah, just wanted to get a head start on the notes," she mumbled. She wasn't sure why, but she felt like she had to prove something today.

Maya raised an eyebrow. "I've known you for years, Leila. You don't do anything without a reason. What's going on?"

Leila sighed and glanced around the room. "It's Destiny," she said quietly. "I feel like we've already got off on the wrong foot, and now it's going to be even worse when we're forced to work together on that project."

Maya tilted her head. "It's not like you to worry about things like this. What's the real problem?"

Leila hesitated, biting her lip. "I just... I don't know. She's been acting like I'm a competition or something, like everything I do, she has to one-up me. I don't know how to deal with that."

Maya smiled gently. "Leila, you've got this. You're one of the most driven people I know. Just show her that you're not intimidated. If she wants to compete, then you'll compete. But don't let her make you feel small."

Leila wasn't convinced, but she appreciated the effort. "Thanks, Maya. I'll try."

The bell rang, and soon enough, Destiny strolled into the room. She was wearing a sharp black jacket and jeans, looking effortlessly put together. Leila felt her stomach flip. She quickly turned her attention to her notebook, pretending to be absorbed in her work.

As Destiny made her way to her seat, she gave Leila a brief glance, but it was cold, almost dismissive. Leila tried not to let it bother her, but the tension was palpable. Her mind raced with what could have been an apology, but the words never came.

Mr. Carter walked in then, breaking the tension. He called out the names of those who would be partners for the upcoming project, and Leila's heart skipped a beat when he said, "Leila and Destiny."

Of course, she thought. There was no escaping it now.

Destiny's eyes flicked up to meet Leila's as they exchanged a brief, awkward glance. Leila felt the weight of the silence between them, unsure of how to break it. Destiny didn't seem eager to engage either, pulling out her notes and starting to organize her things with an air of nonchalance.

"So," Leila started, clearing her throat. "Do you have any ideas for the project?"

Destiny paused, glancing at her briefly. "I'm thinking we should focus on the impact of social media on mental health. It's a popular topic, and I think it'll get a good reaction from the class."

Leila nodded, impressed despite herself. "That's a solid idea. We could break it down into sections—like how social media affects different age groups."

Destiny nodded, tapping her pen against her notebook. "Yeah, we can do that. But I think we'll need some real statistics to back up our points. Something compelling, you know?"

Leila's mind clicked into gear. "What if we got some first-hand accounts? Maybe interview people about how their social media habits have affected their mental health."

Destiny looked at her, a small spark of interest in her eyes. "I like that idea. We can even make a few videos or something to include in the presentation."

Leila felt a small sense of relief. Despite the awkward start, they were making progress. And maybe—just maybe—they could make this work.

Over the next few days, the tension between them started to dissipate, replaced by a strange, tentative teamwork. Destiny wasn't as unbearable as Leila had first assumed, and in return, Leila wasn't as intimidated by Destiny as she had been before. They met up at the library a few times to research and brainstorm, and Leila was surprised to find that Destiny was, in fact, quite intelligent. Her sharp mind, her ability to focus, and her ambition—they weren't things Leila had expected but things she could respect.

Their first real breakthrough came when they managed to track down some statistics on the effects of social media addiction, and Destiny suggested they incorporate the personal stories of people who had experienced these effects firsthand. Leila felt herself warming to the idea of their collaboration, though she didn't let on how much she admired Destiny's quick thinking.

The project was coming together, and as the deadline

approached, they seemed to be more in sync. Leila found herself laughing at Destiny's dry humor, even as she occasionally took the lead in organizing the materials. There was something unexpectedly satisfying about their teamwork, and Leila couldn't help but wonder if maybe there was more to Destiny than she had first thought.

But just as things were starting to look good, the pressure of the project began to take its toll. The night before their presentation, Destiny seemed distant again, her focus turning inward. Leila tried to ask her if everything was okay, but Destiny brushed her off, saying, "I just want to make sure we get this right."

It left Leila feeling unsettled, unsure of what to say. Was Destiny really as invested in this project as she seemed, or was she just pretending for the sake of getting a good grade?

The next day, when they stood in front of the class to present, the air was thick with tension. Leila and Destiny shared a few brief glances, but the unspoken question hung between them. Would they make it through this presentation as a team?

When it was over, Leila felt a mixture of relief and unease. Destiny's smile was tight, but she didn't say much as they packed up their things. It was clear that the awkwardness hadn't disappeared entirely, but for now, they had survived.

As Leila gathered her things, she couldn't shake the feeling that something was off between her and Destiny. The presentation had gone smoothly, but there was a subtle distance in Destiny's behavior that Leila couldn't quite understand. She'd expected a sense of camaraderie after surviving the intense pressure of presenting together, but instead, Destiny seemed withdrawn, like a wall had been placed between them.

"So, that wasn't so bad, right?" Leila ventured, trying to break the silence as they left the classroom.

Destiny's eyes flicked to Leila for a brief moment before looking away again. "Yeah, it was fine," she said, her voice flat.

Leila frowned. "You don't sound convinced. What's up?"

Destiny sighed and paused just before walking out of the classroom. "I don't know, Leila. I guess I just—" She trailed off, clearly struggling to find the words. After a long pause, she continued, "I don't like how people view me when they think I'm working with someone else. Like they see me as weaker, or something. And I don't like that. I don't want anyone to think I can't handle things on my own."

Leila blinked in surprise. She had never thought about Destiny that way. In her mind, Destiny had always been confident, self-assured, someone who had it all together. To hear that she, too, had insecurities made Leila pause. She suddenly felt a pang of guilt for assuming Destiny had everything figured out.

"I didn't know you felt like that," Leila said quietly. "I thought... I thought we were just working together because it made sense. I didn't think it had anything to do with what people thought."

Destiny looked at her, her expression hardening a little. "That's the thing. You don't have to worry about what people think. You're just—you. People don't put that kind of pressure on you the way they do on me. I don't want to let them down. Or you."

Leila's stomach twisted. She hadn't expected this conversation, not in a million years. "Destiny, you don't need to prove anything to anyone. And especially not to me. We did this together, as a team."

Destiny let out a humorless laugh. "I don't know. I just... I don't like having to rely on other people. I guess I'm just not used to it."

The vulnerability in her voice struck a chord with Leila. In a way, Destiny wasn't so different from her. They both had their walls, and their armor, pretending to be something they weren't in order to protect themselves from getting hurt. Leila had never known how much pressure Destiny was under, and the thought made her heart ache.

"Well," Leila said softly, her eyes meeting Destiny's, "if it makes you feel any better, I'm glad we worked together. You might not want to admit it, but you're really good at what you do. I couldn't have done it without you."

Destiny's gaze softened, but only for a moment before her

usual guarded expression returned. "I guess that's true. But it doesn't make it any easier."

Leila wanted to say something more, something to make Destiny feel better, but the words felt inadequate. She didn't have the perfect solution for Destiny's inner conflict, and for the first time, she realized that the person she had thought of as her adversary was just as vulnerable as she was. It was both humbling and unsettling to understand how much they were alike.

The two of them walked silently toward the exit of the school building, each lost in their own thoughts. Leila wasn't sure what to make of everything that had just been said. Could this tension between them be something they could work through? Or would it always exist as an invisible barrier between them?

By the time they reached the gates of the school, the silence was thick, but there was something different about it. It wasn't as uncomfortable as before, but it wasn't exactly comfortable either. It was somewhere in between. Destiny gave Leila a fleeting glance before turning to leave, offering only a curt "See you tomorrow."

Leila watched her go, her mind swirling with a dozen different emotions. She had thought the project would mark a turning point in their relationship—maybe it had, but not in the way she expected.

The next few days were quiet. Destiny and Leila still saw each other in school, but their conversations were few and far between. They'd exchanged a few words in passing, but the vulnerability that had surfaced in their last conversation seemed to hang in the air between them, unspoken and unresolved. Leila found herself wondering if Destiny had thought about what they'd talked about—or if it had simply been another one of those fleeting moments that meant nothing in the grand scheme of things.

Leila tried to focus on other things, like her classes and hanging out with Maya, but her mind kept returning to Destiny. It was hard not to, given how much time they'd spent together on the project. Destiny was on her mind more than she cared to admit, but she didn't know how to bridge the gap between them.

That Friday afternoon, Leila sat alone in the cafeteria,

scrolling through her phone when Maya slid into the seat across from her. "You seem distant today," Maya said, arching an eyebrow.

Leila looked up and shrugged. "Just thinking."

Maya took a bite of her sandwich, clearly uninterested in making small talk. "About?"

Leila hesitated. "About Destiny."

Maya's eyes widened slightly, but she didn't press. Instead, she leaned in a little, her tone softening. "Okay, I know you guys have had your issues, but maybe it's time to stop overthinking it. She's probably feeling just as awkward as you are."

Leila chuckled bitterly. "I don't know, Maya. She's so... closed off. I don't know how to make it better."

"Sometimes you just have to let people be where they are," Maya said gently. "You can't force things to change. If she wants to talk, she will. And if not, well, you'll be okay. You've got your own stuff to focus on."

Leila nodded slowly, feeling a little lighter. Maya had a way of putting things into perspective. Maybe she was right. She couldn't force Destiny to open up or fix everything between them. If Destiny wasn't ready to let go of whatever she was holding onto, then Leila would have to accept it. But that didn't mean she couldn't keep trying to be a friend.

As the bell rang for the end of lunch, Leila stood up, feeling the weight of the day still pressing on her shoulders. But for the first time in a while, she didn't feel so alone in it. Maybe she couldn't fix everything right away, but that didn't mean she had to give up entirely.

And when the next encounter with Destiny came, maybe—just maybe—it would be different.

The weekend passed in a blur of schoolwork and quiet moments. Leila couldn't stop thinking about Destiny. There were moments when she felt the tension, sharp and lingering, but it was also punctuated by memories of those rare, lighthearted exchanges they'd shared. She kept reminding herself that the road to fixing their fractured connection wouldn't be a smooth one, but she wasn't sure where to start.

On Monday morning, Leila arrived at school a little earlier than usual. She was hoping to have some time to herself before the chaos of the day began. She walked through the familiar hallways, glancing at the clock ticking towards the start of the first period, when she noticed Destiny standing by the lockers. She was alone, her hands shoved deep into the pockets of her hoodie, her eyes distant, as though lost in thought.

Leila hesitated for a moment, the old instinct to avoid confrontation tugging at her, but she pushed it aside. This wasn't something that could be avoided forever. She couldn't keep pretending that everything was fine, not when they both knew it wasn't.

Taking a deep breath, she made her way toward Destiny. When Destiny noticed her, there was a slight shift in her expression—a brief moment of surprise, followed by a mask of indifference.

"Hey," Leila said, her voice a little more tentative than she intended.

Destiny didn't immediately respond. Instead, she just nodded, her posture stiff. The silence stretched between them, awkward and uncomfortable. Leila tried not to let the distance make her retreat. She had to push through it.

"I've been thinking about what you said the other day," Leila continued, her words feeling heavier than usual. "About not wanting to rely on anyone. I don't know if I fully get it, but I think I understand, at least a little."

Destiny shifted uncomfortably, looking down at her shoes as if she didn't know how to respond. The vulnerability Leila had seen before seemed to be buried under layers of defensiveness once again.

"You don't have to understand it," Destiny said quietly. "It's just something I've always dealt with. People expect me to be perfect, to always have it together, and sometimes... sometimes it feels like I have to live up to that image, even if it means pushing everyone away."

Leila swallowed hard. She hadn't realized just how much pressure Destiny felt, how much weight she carried silently. It wasn't that Destiny wanted to push her away; it was that she thought she had to. It struck Leila in a way that made her stomach twist. She wanted to help, to ease the tension that seemed to coat every word Destiny spoke, but she didn't know how.

"I think you're allowed to not have it all together," Leila said softly. "You don't have to be perfect, you know? I'm not perfect. And it's okay to lean on people, even if it's hard."

Destiny glanced up, her expression unreadable. The words seemed to hang in the air, their meaning deep but fragile. She didn't respond immediately, and for a moment, Leila thought she might retreat again. But then Destiny sighed and leaned against the locker behind her.

"I don't know how to do that," she admitted. "It feels... wrong, to let people see me as vulnerable. I've always had to be the strong one. The one who doesn't need anyone."

Leila bit her lip, trying to gather her thoughts. "But you don't have to carry everything by yourself. I'm here if you want to talk. I know it's not easy, but I'm not going anywhere."

Destiny's eyes flickered with something like hesitation. Her lips parted, but she closed them again as if weighing her options. There was a long pause before she spoke again, this time her voice a little more fragile than usual.

"I don't want to drag you down, Leila. I've already messed things up between us, and I don't know how to fix that."

Leila shook her head quickly. "You haven't messed anything up. You've just been... struggling. And that's okay. You don't have to fix everything right away. I just want to be here for you. To be your friend."

Destiny blinked, as though the weight of those words took a moment to sink in. "You mean it?" she asked softly, almost as if she wasn't sure she could trust the sincerity behind them.

Leila smiled gently. "Of course, I do. We're friends. I know we've had our moments, but I'm not going anywhere. I want to be here, even if it means taking things slow."

For a second, Destiny looked vulnerable—like she was standing on the edge of something, unsure whether to jump or turn back. But the walls in her eyes softened, just a little, and Leila could see the faintest trace of relief in her expression.

"Okay," Destiny said, her voice quieter now, like the tension had been drained out of it. "I'll... I'll try."

It wasn't an instant change, and Leila didn't expect it to be. But as the bell rang, signaling the start of the first period, she felt something shift—something fragile but important, like the start of a new chapter.

They walked together to class, the silence between them not as heavy as before. Destiny didn't look quite as distant, and Leila felt a tentative sense of hope. Maybe it wouldn't be easy, but maybe, just maybe, they could work through this.

As the day went on, the interactions between them felt a little less strained. They shared brief moments between classes, and exchanged a few words here and there, and though the distance hadn't fully disappeared, there was a quiet understanding beginning to form. Leila found herself hoping that this was the beginning of something different—not necessarily perfect, but real. Something that wasn't built on expectations, but on honesty.

That afternoon, as the school day ended and the final bell rang, Leila stood by her locker, organizing her things. She felt a tap on her shoulder and turned to see Destiny standing there, a small smile on her face. It was hesitant, but it was there.

"Hey," Destiny said, looking a little awkward. "I know it's still... not easy, but thanks. For not giving up on me."

Leila's heart swelled with something warm. "I'm not going anywhere, Destiny. You don't have to do this alone."

And for the first time in a long while, Destiny looked like she believed it.

With that, they walked out of school together, side by side, the unspoken tension between them finally beginning to fade. It wasn't a perfect moment, but it was a real one. And Leila felt like they were finally on the path toward something better.

The next few days weren't perfect, and Leila didn't expect them to be. There were still moments of silence, moments when Destiny seemed withdrawn or lost in her own thoughts. But there were also small victories. They shared a few laughs between classes, and talked about their shared interests more than they had in months, and slowly, Leila felt like she was breaking through the walls Destiny had built around herself.

One afternoon, as the two of them sat on the steps outside the school, Leila could feel the change in the air. The weather was warmer, the kind of spring day that seemed to breathe new life into everything. Destiny had her sketchbook open, flipping through pages with absentminded movements, while Leila worked on a math problem that she had been struggling with. The quiet between them felt comfortable now like they didn't have to fill every second with conversation. It was the kind of silence that spoke of understanding, of knowing each other's company didn't need to be forced.

Leila glanced at Destiny and noticed the way her eyes softened as she looked at her sketch. The familiar lines and curves of the art that always seemed to flow from her pen were no longer as harsh as they had been. They were lighter, and smoother, almost as though Destiny's mood was starting to reflect in her art. Leila admired that about her—how her creativity bled into her emotions, how she could translate everything she felt onto the page.

"Hey," Leila began, breaking the silence. "You know, I've been thinking about what you said... about not wanting to rely on anyone."

Destiny didn't look up at first, but she nodded as though she was anticipating where this was going. "Yeah?"

Leila hesitated. She knew this wasn't going to be easy, but if they were going to make this work, they needed to keep having these tough conversations. "I think it's okay to rely on people sometimes, Destiny. You don't have to carry everything by yourself. I don't want to be someone you have to push away."

Destiny didn't respond immediately. Instead, she closed her sketchbook, the sudden motion drawing Leila's full attention. "I don't know how to do that," she said, her voice quieter than before. "It's hard for me to let people in."

Leila's heart went out to her. She could see it now—the hesitancy, the vulnerability that Destiny had buried beneath layers of sarcasm and distance. It wasn't that Destiny didn't want to connect; it was that she had been hurt before, had been let down too many times, and had learned to keep everyone at arm's length.

"You don't have to do it all at once," Leila said gently. "You don't have to let me in completely if you're not ready. But I'm here, and I'll be patient. I just want you to know that you're not alone, okay?"

Destiny's eyes flickered, a mixture of doubt and something else—something softer that she rarely let anyone see. After a long pause, she sighed and nodded. "Okay. I'll try. But... don't expect me to be an open book all of a sudden."

Leila smiled. "I wouldn't dream of it. But I'm not going anywhere. One step at a time."

For the rest of the afternoon, the two of them stayed there, enjoying the unspoken comfort of each other's company. Leila had a feeling that Destiny's walls weren't going to crumble overnight, but she also knew that this was a start—a real start.

The following week, things continued to improve, though slowly. They began walking to class together more often, talking about trivial things—schoolwork, gossip, music—and occasionally, Destiny would let a bit of her vulnerability slip through, though she was careful to keep it hidden most of the time.

One day, after history class, Destiny surprised Leila by asking if she wanted to walk home with her. It wasn't a huge gesture, but it felt significant, like an invitation into a part of her world that Leila hadn't been allowed to enter before. Leila, of course, accepted, and the two of them started walking through the neighborhood together, talking about anything and everything. For the first time in months, Leila felt like she was walking alongside her best friend, not the distant, hardened version of Destiny that had kept her at arm's length for so long.

As they neared Leila's house, Destiny hesitated, her hands shoved into her hoodie pockets as she looked at the pavement. "Leila," she began quietly, "I just wanted to say thanks. For not giving up on me. For not thinking I was too much."

Leila stopped walking for a moment and turned to face her, surprised by the sincerity in Destiny's voice. "Of course. I told you, I'm not going anywhere. I don't want you to feel like you have to push me away."

Destiny met her gaze, and for a brief moment, the walls she'd built around herself seemed to lower, just a fraction. "I think... I think I'm learning how to trust people again," she said, her voice almost a whisper. "It's hard, but I want to try."

Leila smiled, feeling a warmth spread through her chest. "That's all I ask. And I'll be here, no matter what."

They continued walking, their steps in sync as they made their way through the familiar streets. Leila couldn't help but feel hopeful. There was still a long road ahead, and there would undoubtedly be moments of setback. But for the first time in a long while, she felt like she and Destiny were headed in the right direction. One step at a time.

As they reached Leila's house, Destiny stopped at the end of the driveway, an unspoken question hanging in the air. "I'll see you tomorrow?" she asked.

Leila nodded, her smile genuine. "Yeah, I'll see you tomorrow."

And as Destiny turned and walked down the street, Leila felt a quiet sense of satisfaction settle over her. It wasn't perfect, not by a long shot, but it was real. And for now, that was enough.

The days that followed were a quiet storm of small changes between Leila and Destiny. They continued to grow more comfortable with each other, but the journey wasn't easy. There were moments when Destiny would pull away, retreating into herself, and Leila couldn't help but wonder if maybe she was pushing too hard. But she never stopped trying. There were other times when Destiny would crack a smile, or share a random thought, and Leila would feel a sense of warmth spread through her, knowing that she was slowly making a difference.

It was a Wednesday afternoon when it all came to a head. The weather had turned warmer, the days growing longer as spring finally arrived in full force. The two of them were sitting in their usual spot at lunch, a quiet bench near the side of the school, where no one else ever seemed to sit. Leila had her lunch spread out, while Destiny was absentmindedly drawing patterns on the table, her pencil tapping against the wood in a steady rhythm.

"So," Leila said, her voice casual but carrying a weight of curiosity. "I've been meaning to ask... how do you deal with everything?"

Destiny paused, her pencil hovering above the table for a moment before she glanced up at Leila, a look in her eyes that was equal parts wary and thoughtful.

"Everything?" Destiny repeated, a frown tugging at her lips.

Leila nodded. "Yeah, you know... everything that's been going on. The pressure, the uncertainty... I mean, you've been through a lot, and you just... keep it all inside."

Destiny's expression darkened, the walls coming back up faster than Leila could blink. She was quiet for a long time, just staring at the table as though she could read the grains of the wood. Leila held her breath, wondering if she'd made a mistake by asking, but she refused to back down. Destiny was hurting, and Leila had a front-row seat to her pain, whether or not she was ready to show it.

Finally, Destiny spoke, her voice low and rough. "I don't talk about it because no one really listens. People say they do, but they don't. And when you let people in... they just let you down eventually."

Leila's heart twisted at the bitterness in her voice. She couldn't understand it fully, not yet, but she knew enough to knowthat Destiny's walls were not just about pride or stubbornness. There was something deeper, something that had caused her to build this fortress around herself. And Leila wanted—no, needed—to understand it.

"I get that," Leila said softly, her tone measured. "I do. But not everyone is like that, Destiny. I'm not like that. I'm not going anywhere. I promise."

Destiny looked up at her, her expression unreadable for a long time. For a moment, Leila thought she might see some flicker of doubt in her eyes, some acknowledgment that she wanted to believe her, but it was quickly replaced by something else.

Something colder.

"You don't know what it's like," Destiny muttered. "To just... feel like you're constantly running on empty, like everyone expects something from you but no one ever gives anything back."

Leila sat up straighter, feeling the weight of Destiny's words. She wanted to say something comforting, something that would make Destiny feel heard, but she knew it wouldn't be enough. Destiny had been carrying this burden for so long, and Leila wasn't sure how to take that weight off her shoulders.

"I can't imagine what that's like," Leila said, her voice gentle, "but I do know this: you don't have to keep running. You don't have to keep carrying all that alone."

For a brief, fleeting moment, it seemed as though Destiny was about to say something more. Her lips parted as if she wanted to respond, but then she closed her mouth again, pulling her sketchbook toward her like a shield.

"I'm fine," she said, her voice hardening once more. "I don't need anyone's help."

Leila didn't press further. She knew better than to push too hard. Destiny would come around when she was ready, and inthe meantime, all Leila could do was be there. She picked up her own lunch, the moment slipping into uncomfortable silence as they ate. Destiny was quiet, lost in her thoughts, her eyes never meeting Leila's. Leila's stomach tightened, but she didn't say anything.

Just before the bell rang to signal the end of lunch, Destiny stood up abruptly, slinging her bag over her shoulder. "I have to go," she said, her tone clipped.

Leila didn't try to stop her, didn't try to convince her to stay. She knew better now. Instead, she just gave a soft, "Okay. I'll see you later."

And then Destiny was gone, walking away with that same steady pace, head down, shoulders hunched. Leila watched her go, a mixture of hope and frustration swelling in her chest. She wanted to fix everything, to make Destiny see that she didn't have to be alone, that she didn't have to keep all her hurt inside. But she also knew that Destiny had to want that change for herself. All Leila could do was wait. And maybe, in time, Destiny would let her in.

The rest of the day passed in a blur, each class a dull echo in Leila's mind as she replayed the conversation over and over.She couldn't help but wonder if she had said the wrong things if she had pushed too hard. But then again, she thought, maybe this was just part of the process. Maybe it was just one of those moments where things got worse before they got better. She could only hope.

When the final bell rang, signaling the end of the school day, Leila grabbed her bag and headed for the doors, feeling the weight of the conversation still lingering in the air. She was about to step outside when she heard someone call her name.

"Leila!"

She turned, startled, and saw Destiny standing a few feet away, her hands shoved into her pockets. She was looking at the ground, but there was something different in her posture, something more open than before.

Leila's heart skipped a beat. "Destiny?"

The other girl hesitated for a moment before meeting her gaze. "I'm sorry," Destiny said, her voice quieter than usual. "I didn't mean to shut you out. I... just get scared sometimes. I don't know how to do this."

Leila smiled, her heart lifting at the words she had been waiting for. "It's okay. I get it. And I'm still here. Whenever you're ready."

Destiny nodded, her lips tugging into a tentative smile. It wasn't much, but it was a start. And for Leila, that was more than enough.

Leila could hardly believe the shift in Destiny. Her heart was racing with both excitement and uncertainty as they stood there in the school courtyard, the evening sun casting long shadows across the pavement. Destiny was finally letting down some of the walls she had so carefully constructed, and while Leila knew the process would take time, it felt like a huge victory.

"I don't know how to... let people in," Destiny admitted, her voice soft but steady now. She was looking at the ground again, her fingers toying with the strap of her bag. "It's not something

I can just... turn off. You know?"

Leila nodded, understanding more than she could put into words. She knew that, at the heart of it, Destiny's fear wasn't rooted in distrust but in the deep scars from a past that still haunted her. It wasn't something that could be fixed overnight, and Leila wasn't going to rush it. She was patient—she could be patient for Destiny.

"I know," Leila said, her voice calm and unwavering. "But you don't have to do it all alone. You've got me now."

Destiny's eyes flickered up at that, a flash of vulnerability crossing her face before she quickly masked it again. Leila wasn't sure if she had fully accepted what she had just said, but the fact that Destiny was still standing there, still talking, made her hopeful.

"I'll try," Destiny murmured after a moment, finally looking up at Leila, her eyes meeting hers. "But I don't know if I can... trust people that easily."

Leila's smile was gentle, not pushing, just offering. "Take it slow. We can take it one step at a time. We don't have to rush anything."

Destiny nodded slowly as if the words were sinking in. There was a long pause, and for a moment, neither of them spoke. The silence between them was comfortable, filled with the kind of unspoken understanding that often came from sharing space with someone who genuinely cared. It was something Leila hadn't realized she needed, something she hadn't had with many people before.

As they started walking out of the school gates, Destiny fell into step beside Leila, the tension between them gradually melting away. The air was warm, the smell of freshly cut grass lingering in the breeze as they made their way toward the bus stop. Destiny kept her eyes ahead, but her pace was more relaxed, less rigid than before. Leila could tell that she was still holding a lot inside, but this—this small crack in the wall—was a start.

They made small talk as they walked, their conversation flowing in fits and starts, but it was more than Leila had ever expected from Destiny. She realized that despite the surface-level distance, there was more to Destiny than she had initially thought. Underneath the layers of sarcasm, indifference, and isolation, there was a person who just wanted to be understood, just like anyone else.

When they reached the bus stop, Destiny was the first to sit down on the bench, her posture still somewhat guarded but not as tense as it had been earlier. Leila sat next to her, the weight of the quiet between them settling again, though this time it didn't feel heavy. It felt like something different—like a moment of peace.

"I don't know if I can make any promises," Destiny said quietly, breaking the silence. "But I'll try to let you in. Just... don't expect me to be all sunshine and rainbows, okay? I'm not... like that."

Leila grinned, her heart swelling at the honesty in Destiny's voice. "I don't expect you to be perfect. Just... be you."

Destiny's lips twitched in what might have been the beginning of a smile. "Yeah, well... I'm not sure if 'me' is someone you want to get too close to."

Leila turned to look at her, her smile softening. "I think you're underestimating yourself."

Destiny met her gaze, her eyes narrowing slightly in disbelief, but there was a glimmer of something—maybe curiosity, maybe a flicker of hope. It was fleeting, but Leila saw it.

The bus pulled up then, its engine rumbling as the doors swung open. Leila stood up, and Destiny followed, still walking a little behind her, as though she wasn't quite ready to take that step forward. Leila waited, making sure that Destiny didn't feel rushed, and once the two of them were on board and settled into their seats, the world around them seemed to slow down.

The ride to Destiny's stop was quiet, but this time, it wasn't uncomfortable. Destiny stared out the window, but Leila didn't mind. Sometimes, silence wasn't something to fill—it was something to appreciate. She knew now that their relationship wouldn't be about grand gestures or constant conversation. It would be about these small moments, where both of them could just exist side by side and know that the other person was there, without expectation or pressure.

As the bus came to a stop at Destiny's house, she stood up quickly, making her way to the door. Leila followed, moving more slowly, and as Destiny stepped off the bus, she turned to face Leila for just a moment.

"Thanks for being here," Destiny said softly, her voice quieter than usual. "I'm not sure if I'm ready for all this... but it means a lot that you're still sticking around."

Leila smiled, feeling a surge of warmth. "I'll always stick around," she said firmly. "We'll figure it out, one day at a time."

Destiny looked at her for a moment longer, something unreadable in her eyes, before nodding and walking away, disappearing into the distance.

Leila watched her go, a sense of satisfaction settling deep in her chest. She didn't have all the answers. She didn't know what the future held for their friendship, or even if they'd be able to navigate all the complexities that came with it. But she knew one thing for sure: this was just the beginning. Destiny was starting to trust her, and Leila was going to be patient, to hold space for her, as long as it took.

As the bus drove off and the noise of the city surrounded her, Leila couldn't help but smile to herself. She had done something right, even if it was just one small step. And maybe that was all she needed to keep going.

Chapter 3
Breaking the Silence

The week flew by quicker than Leila had anticipated. Between the usual hustle of school and work, she found herself thinking about Destiny more than she had expected. Her mind replayed their conversation over and over, wondering if she had said the right things and if she had truly helped Destiny take even the smallest step toward opening up. She wasn't sure yet if that moment on the bus was a breakthrough or just a temporary crack in the wall Destiny had built around herself. Either way, Leila couldn't help but feel a sense of accomplishment, even if it was fleeting.

By Friday, though, things felt different. Destiny had been absent from school on Wednesday and Thursday, and Leila couldn't shake the nagging worry that she'd done something wrong, that maybe she had pushed too hard. The longer she went without hearing from Destiny, the more anxious she became. Her text messages went unanswered, and the silence felt heavier each day. Maybe Destiny had changed her mind about letting anyone in, or maybe she was regretting the conversation. Leila didn't know.

It was Friday afternoon when Leila received a text from Destiny, the simple message reading, Can we talk after school?Leila's stomach fluttered with both excitement and anxiety. She didn't hesitate; she quickly typed back, Of course. Where?

Destiny's reply came quickly, By the bleachers.

When school let out, Leila practically ran to the bleachers. Her heart was beating faster with each step, her mind racing through a hundred scenarios. Was Destiny going to apologize? Was she going to tell Leila she wasn't ready to try again? Or maybe, just maybe, Destiny was going to show up and surprise her in a way that would make everything make sense. Leila had no idea, but she was determined to find out.

As she reached the bleachers, she spotted Destiny sitting alone at the very top, her back turned, her shoulders slumped in a way that suggested she was deep in thought. Leila took a deep breath, feeling the weight of the moment settle on her. She climbed the steps and slowly made her way to where Destiny was sitting, her presence now unmistakable.

"Hey," Leila said softly, standing beside Destiny. Her voice felt strangely quiet against the backdrop of the empty schoolyard.

Destiny looked up at her, her dark eyes guarded but not as closed off as they had been before. She didn't say anything at first, just looked at Leila with an expression that was hard to read.

"Can we sit down?" Leila asked gently, nodding toward the space next to Destiny.

Destiny hesitated for a moment, but then slowly patted the space beside her. Leila sat down, not too close, but just enough to show that she was there—ready, as always, to listen.

"I've been thinking," Destiny began, her voice quieter than usual. "About what we talked about last week. About... letting people in." She took a deep breath before continuing. "I've been shutting people out for so long, Leila. It's just... easier that way, you know? If I keep everyone at arm's length, then they can't hurt me. I can't get hurt if I don't let anyone get too close."

Leila nodded, her heart aching as she listened to Destiny's

words. She knew how hard it was for Destiny to say these things, to admit that the walls she had built were not just out of anger or stubbornness, but out of fear. It made sense to Leila, in a way that it hadn't before.

"I understand," Leila said softly, her voice filled with empathy. "It's easier to protect yourself, but that doesn't mean it's healthy. It doesn't mean you have to keep doing it."

Destiny glanced over at Leila, her expression still cautious, but there was a softness in her eyes that hadn't been there before. "I don't know how to stop, though," she admitted. "It's like... a reflex, you know? I don't even think about it anymore. I just push people away."

"I get it," Leila said, her heart reaching out to Destiny in a way that words couldn't fully express. "But you don't have to do it alone anymore. You've got me, Destiny. I'll be here, no matter what. You don't have to push me away."

Destiny's lips trembled for a moment as if the weight of her emotions were threatening to spill over. She blinked rapidly, looking away for a second as though trying to collect herself. But when she finally looked back at Leila, there was a small, hesitant smile on her face.

"Thank you," she whispered. "I don't know if I'm ready, but... I'll try. For you. And for me."

Leila smiled back, her chest swelling with a mixture of pride and hope. It was a small step, but it was a step, and that was more than she had ever expected from Destiny. She could see the struggle in Destiny's eyes, the internal battle between what she knew was safe—staying closed off—and the unfamiliar feeling of allowing someone in.

"Take your time," Leila said gently. "There's no rush. I'm not going anywhere."

The two of them sat in silence for a while, the quiet between them no longer feeling strained, but peaceful. Leila didn't push; she just let Destiny be, knowing that the moment was important for both of them. Destiny needed to process, and Leila needed to be patient.

Eventually, Destiny spoke again, her voice steady. "I think

I've been afraid for a long time. Afraid of letting someone in, afraid of what might happen if I do." She paused, looking at the ground for a moment, and when she looked up again, her eyes were filled with something that Leila could only describe as vulnerability. "But I want to try, Leila. I want to try to trust you."

Leila felt her heart skip a beat. She hadn't expected those words to come from Destiny, but they hit her harder than anything else she had heard. It was a promise, small but significant. And even though Destiny wasn't fully ready, she was beginning to let go of her fear.

"I'm glad," Leila said, her voice filled with sincerity. "You don't have to do anything you're not ready for, but I'm reallyglad you're willing to try."

Destiny nodded slowly, her lips curving into a small, genuine smile. "Yeah," she murmured. "Me too."

As the sun began to set, casting a golden glow over the bleachers, Leila felt a sense of peace settle inside her. She knew the road ahead wouldn't always be easy. There would be moments when Destiny would pull away again, moments when Leila would feel like she was losing ground. But for now, this—this moment—was enough. It was more than enough.

Leila walked beside Destiny through the bustling halls of their high school, the noise of students and lockers slamming shut washing over them like a wave. The air was thick with the usual chatter, but for the first time in a while, Leila felt oddly out of place. It wasn't the typical tension of being an outsider—it was different, more subtle. Destiny was beside her, but there was a distance between them, a small gap that hadn't been there before.

She glanced at Destiny, who was walking a little ahead of her, head down, the usual confident swagger now absent. Leila couldn't help but wonder what was going on inside her friend's mind. They hadn't really spoken about what happened the night before—the almost fight, the sharp words, the accusations. Leila felt the weight of it in her chest, like a stone lodged there. She was ready to move past it, but she wasn't sure if Destiny was.

"Hey, you good?" Leila asked quietly, matching Destiny's pace.

Destiny stopped walking and turned to face her, her expression unreadable. She looked different today—less put-together, less like the girl who'd always seemed to have it all figured out. There was something vulnerable in her eyes that Leila hadn't seen before.

"I'm fine," Destiny said, but her voice lacked conviction.

Leila could feel the tension building again, the same quiet unease that had hung between them since that night. She didn't know how to fix it—didn't even know if it could be fixed. She could feel the distance, growing just a little bit more with each passing moment.

Destiny's eyes flickered down the hall, avoiding Leila's gaze. "I'm sorry," she said suddenly, her voice softer now, almost too quiet. "About last night. I shouldn't have—"

Leila held up her hand, cutting her off. "Don't. It's okay. We don't need to go over it again."

But Destiny shook her head, her dark curls bouncing around her face. "No, it's not okay. You were right. I've been acting like everything's fine, but it's not. And I've been shutting you out, Leila, and that's not fair to you."

Leila blinked, surprised by the honesty in Destiny's voice. She'd always been the confident one, the girl who took charge and had an answer for everything. To hear her admit that she'd been wrong felt like a quiet shift like something was finally starting to break through the walls Destiny had built around herself.

"You don't have to apologize," Leila said, her voice softer now, understanding slipping into her tone. "We've both been kind of... off lately. I just—" She hesitated. "I don't know. I didn't want to push you away."

Destiny's eyes met hers then, really met hers, and for the first time in a long while, Leila saw something like real emotion in them—raw, unfiltered. "I'm scared, Leila," she said, her voice barely above a whisper.

Leila frowned, confused. "Scared of what?"

Destiny's gaze flickered down to the floor before she took a deep breath and met Leila's eyes again. "I'm scared of losing everything. Of losing you. I've been so focused on trying to be perfect, trying to keep everything together, but it's exhausting. And the more I push you away, the more it feels like I'm losing control."

Leila felt a wave of sympathy wash over her. She had always known Destiny as the girl who had it all figured out, who seemed to never worry about anything, but now she was seeing her in a different light. Destiny was scared. She was just like everyone else, struggling to keep up with the chaos around her.

Leila took a step closer, closing the gap between them. "I'm not going anywhere, okay?" she said, her voice steady. "I'm here. You don't have to do this alone."

Destiny's lips trembled slightly, and Leila could see the fight in her eyes—like she was holding herself back from letting go. And then, without warning, Destiny stepped forward and wrapped her arms around Leila, pulling her into a hug. It was a tight hug, almost desperate like she had been waiting for this moment for too long.

Leila froze at first, but then she relaxed into the embrace, letting herself feel the comfort of being there, of knowing that maybe, just maybe, everything was going to be okay.

"I'm sorry I've been such a mess," Destiny muttered into Leila's shoulder. "I didn't mean to push you away. I just... didn't know how to deal with everything."

Leila smiled, rubbing her friend's back in slow circles. "You don't have to apologize. We're in this together, right?"

Destiny pulled back slightly, wiping her eyes with the back of her hand. "Right," she said, her voice thick with emotion.

For a moment, neither of them spoke. They just stood there, letting the weight of the last few weeks settle in between them. It wasn't perfect—it was messy and complicated and still full of uncertainties—but it was real. And that was enough for now.

The bell rang, signaling the end of lunch, and they both looked up, startled by how much time had passed. Destiny gave a small laugh, almost embarrassed.

"Guess we should get to class," she said, her usual confidence starting to return.

Leila nodded, her heart lighter than it had been in days. "Yeah, guess so."

They started walking back to the hallway, their steps in sync, and for the first time in what felt like forever, Leila felt like they were finally back on the same page.

She didn't know what the future held for them, but at that moment, it didn't matter. They had broken the silence. And maybe, just maybe, that was the beginning of something new.

The rest of the day seemed to drift by in a blur. Leila could barely focus on her classes. Her mind kept circling back to the conversation with Destiny. The way she'd opened up. The vulnerability in her voice. Leila had never seen her friend like that before, and it left her feeling a mix of awe and confusion. Was this the start of something new between them? Or was it just a moment of weakness on Destiny's part?

Leila had always known Destiny to be tough, almost impenetrable, the kind of person who carried herself with confidence and assuredness. She didn't let anything break her down. But today, for the first time, she'd seen cracks in that façade—real, raw cracks.

By the time the final bell rang, signaling the end of the school day, Leila was both exhausted and relieved. She needed some time to process everything. She wasn't sure how she felt about Destiny's apology—it was like a weight had been lifted, but at the same time, the air between them felt thick with unspoken words.

Leila gathered her things quickly and headed out the door, hoping to avoid the chaos of the crowded hallways. But as she was about to slip out of the school's main entrance, she felt a familiar hand on her shoulder.

"Hey, wait up!"

She turned to find Destiny jogging toward her, her backpack bouncing against her back. Her face was flushed from the rush, and there was a nervous energy about her that made Leila pause.

"I wanted to talk," Destiny said, a little out of breath.

Leila raised an eyebrow. "About?"

"About... everything. I don't know. I just—I don't want things to be weird between us anymore." Destiny's voice wavered slightly, and it was clear she was struggling to find the right words.

Leila took a deep breath. She had already given Destiny her forgiveness, but this conversation felt like the next step in fixing what had been broken. "Okay. I'm listening."

They sat down on the steps just outside the school, the late afternoon sun casting long shadows over the pavement. For a moment, neither of them said anything. It felt like they were both waiting for the other to speak first, but the silence was heavy, filled with too much unsaid.

Finally, Destiny spoke, her words slow and careful. "I guess... I've been pushing you away for a while now. Not just lately, but for a long time. You probably already knew that, huh?"

Leila nodded, though she didn't speak. She had known—she just hadn't understood why.

Destiny continued, her gaze focused on the ground in front of them. "I don't know why I do it. I guess it's just easier. I always thought if I kept people at arm's length, I wouldn't get hurt. But then... you came along, and it was different. You actually made me want to let someone in, you know? And then I got scared. I guess I'm scared of depending on anyone. Scared of things changing."

Leila was quiet for a long moment, processing her friend's words. "I get that," she finally said, her voice soft. "I think I've been scared too, in a way. It's not always easy to let someone close."

Destiny glanced at her then, a faint smile tugging at the corner of her lips. "I'm glad you understand. It feels like I've been running away from everything, and I'm so tired of it."

Leila could see the sincerity in Destiny's eyes, and it gave her a sense of relief. Maybe it wasn't too late for them. Maybe there was still hope for their friendship.

"But," Leila began, choosing her words carefully, "you can't just expect everything to go back to normal overnight. You've hurt me too, Destiny. I've been feeling like I didn't matter to you anymore."

Destiny's face dropped, and Leila saw the guilt settle in her eyes. "I never wanted to make you feel that way. You're my best friend, Leila. You always have been. I just... I don't know what I was thinking."

Leila sighed. "I know. I get it now. I just—I need time. We both do. I don't want to rush back into things, you know?"

Destiny nodded, her expression softening. "I'm okay with that. I don't expect everything to magically fix itself. I just want to make sure you know that I'm here, and I want to try again. I want us to be okay."

Leila's heart warmed at the sincerity in her friend's voice. Maybe, just maybe, this was the beginning of something new. Not a perfect friendship, but one that could be rebuilt—one step at a time.

"I think we'll be okay," Leila said quietly, a small smile breaking through. "It's going to take time, but we'll figure it out."

Destiny smiled back, a weight lifting from her shoulders. "Thank you. For understanding. I promise I'll work on it."

The two girls sat in comfortable silence for a while, just taking in the quiet of the evening. It was the first time in weeks that Leila felt like she could breathe easy around Destiny like they weren't caught in an endless loop of miscommunication and unspoken tension. For the first time, she felt like there was a chance for things to get better.

As the sun began to dip below the horizon, painting the sky in hues of pink and orange, Leila stood up, brushing off her jeans. "You ready to head home?"

Destiny stood as well, stretching her arms above her head. "Yeah. Let's go."

They walked side by side down the steps, the sound of their footsteps in sync with one another, and for the first time in a long while, the air between them didn't feel heavy. There was still work to be done, but maybe, just maybe, they were finally on the right path.

As they walked off into the evening, the promise of a fresh start hung in the air, and for the first time in weeks, Leila felt hopeful. The road ahead wouldn't be easy, but it was one she was willing to walk—together with Destiny.

The days that followed seemed to pass in a blur, but there was a noticeable shift between Leila and Destiny. The tension that had once filled every interaction was gradually replaced by something gentler. A tentative understanding. They were still figuring things out, but it felt different now—more hopeful, more real.

Leila found herself replaying their conversation from that afternoon over and over in her mind. Destiny's confession, her vulnerability—it had been a side of her that Leila hadn't seen before. It made her rethink everything. Destiny had always been the one to keep her guard up, to make people think she was untouchable. It was strange, but it made Leila feel like maybe, just maybe, their friendship could survive this storm after all.

Despite this small sense of relief, Leila couldn't shake the lingering thought that there was still something they hadn't addressed. She'd forgiven Destiny, but it wasn't enough. Not yet. Not when everything they'd been through together hung between them like an unresolved question.

It wasn't until the following weekend that they had another heart-to-heart. Leila had been at home, staring out her window at the pale morning sky when her phone buzzed. It was a message from Destiny.

"Hey, do you want to hang out? I've been thinking about what we talked about the other day, and I think we need to clear the air more. If you're up for it."

Leila paused, her finger hovering over the screen as she thought about it. Part of her wanted to push it aside and pretend everything was fine. But deep down, she knew she couldn't. Not yet. They couldn't just ignore what had happened. It was too big, too important.

"Yeah, sure. I'm free in a bit. Let's meet at the park?"

A few seconds later, Destiny's reply came through.

"Sounds good. See you soon."

Leila grabbed her jacket and headed out the door. The crisp air hit her face as soon as she stepped outside, and she pulled her sleeves down over her hands for warmth. The walk to the park wasn't long—just a few blocks—but it gave her time to think. She couldn't help but wonder what kind of conversation they were going to have this time. Was it going to be awkward? Would they slip back into old habits of avoiding the hard conversations? Or would they finally make real progress?

When she arrived at the park, she spotted Destiny immediately. She was sitting on one of the benches near the small pond, her dark hair falling in waves around her shoulders, a quiet intensity in her posture. It was clear that Destiny had been waiting for this moment just as much as Leila had.

Leila approached cautiously, unsure of how to start the conversation. She didn't want to say the wrong thing, didn't want to make Destiny feel like she was pressuring her. But at the same time, she knew that if they didn't talk now, they might never get the chance to truly understand each other.

Destiny glanced up when she heard Leila's footsteps, a small, uncertain smile spreading across her face. "Hey."

"Hey," Leila replied, sitting down beside her. The air between them felt thick and heavy with unsaid words. "I'm glad you messaged me."

Destiny nodded, pulling her knees to her chest and wrapping her arms around them. "I've been thinking about what we said the other day. And... I feel like we need to really talk. Not just about the apology, but about everything. Why do we let things get so bad."

Leila swallowed, the words hitting her with more weight than she expected. "I agree. I think we both knew something wasn't right, but I don't think we knew how to fix it. Or if we even could."

Destiny met her gaze, her eyes dark with emotion. "I'm sorry for shutting you out, Leila. I should've talked to you sooner. I should've told you what was going on in my head instead of just pulling away. I never meant to hurt you."

Leila took a deep breath, her heart aching at the sincerity in Destiny's voice. "I know you didn't mean to hurt me. But you did. And I think... I think I hurt you, too. I've been trying so hard to keep everything together, to pretend like nothing was wrong. But it was. And I didn't know how to tell you that I felt like I was losing you."

Destiny's expression softened, and she reached over, resting a hand on Leila's arm. "I didn't mean to make you feel that way. You mean everything to me. You're my best friend, Leila. I was just... scared. Scared of everything changing, scared of losing you. And I didn't know how to deal with that, so I pushed you away."

Leila nodded, feeling the sting of those words deep inside her. She could relate—her own fears and her own insecurities had made her do things she wasn't proud of too. But hearing Destiny admit it so openly made her feel less alone.

"I was scared too," Leila said softly. "I've been holding onto the idea that everything has to stay the same, that things can't change. But they do. They always do. And sometimes, we have to let go of the old versions of ourselves to move forward."

There was a long pause as the words hung between them, heavy with their implications. But it wasn't uncomfortable. It was the kind of silence that came after understanding. The kind of silence that signaled something new, something better was on the horizon.

"You're right," Destiny said, breaking the silence at last. "Things have changed. But maybe that's not such a bad thing. Maybe it's just part of growing up."

Leila smiled at her friend, her heart lightening just a little. "Yeah. Maybe it is."

The two girls sat there for a while longer, talking about everything and nothing. They laughed, joked, and shared stories—things that felt so natural, so familiar. It was like no time had passed at all like they were back to the way things were before. But this time, it felt real. It felt like they were rebuilding something strong.

As the sun began to set, casting a warm glow across the park, Leila realized something. She wasn't afraid anymore. They'd faced their issues head-on, and while things weren't perfect, they were moving in the right direction. For the first time in a long time, Leila felt like she was truly seeing Destiny—not just as her best friend, but as someone who had her own struggles, her own fears. And in return, she felt like Destiny was finally seeing her for who she was.

"We'll be okay," Leila said, the words slipping out before she could stop them.

Destiny nodded, her eyes glinting with something new—something hopeful. "Yeah. I think we will."

As they sat together in the fading light, the weight of the conversation slowly started to lift. Destiny let out a long breath and stretched her legs out in front of her, breaking the comfortable silence between them.

"You know, I never thought we'd be able to get past this," Destiny said, a wistful smile crossing her face. "I thought I'd messed everything up beyond repair. But I guess I was wrong."

Leila shifted, looking over at her, a soft chuckle escaping her lips. "I think we both thought that, at one point. It was easier to imagine it was all falling apart rather than figuring out how to fix it."

"Yeah," Destiny admitted, glancing away for a moment, her gaze distant. "I just didn't know how to make it better. Or if it even could be."

Leila nodded, understanding the depth of her words. Sometimes, when a relationship, whether friendship or otherwise, goes through a rocky period, it's easy to think there's no coming back. You fall into the trap of believing that the damage is irreversible and that the cracks can never be filled. But today, she realized that wasn't true. They had been through a rough patch, and while things weren't completely healed, they had made a choice to work on it. That was enough.

"It's kind of strange, though," Leila said after a pause, her voice quieter now. "We've been friends for so long, but we've never really talked like this before. It always felt like there were things we kept to ourselves, things we never addressed."

Destiny glanced at her, raising an eyebrow. "You mean like the fact that we've been skating around each other's feelings for months?"

Leila laughed, a small, self-deprecating sound. "Yeah, that. I don't know why we did that. It just feels like... we should have known better, you know?"

Destiny shrugged, the smile on her face softening. "Maybe it was just easier to pretend. Easier to keep everything inside rather than risk making things worse. But here we are now. We're still talking. And that's what matters."

Leila couldn't help but agree. It was strange, this newfound vulnerability between them. There had always been a wall between them, one built out of their individual insecurities and the fear of being rejected. It wasn't something either of them had been aware of until now. But now that it had been acknowledged, it seemed easier to see a future where they could be open with one another, without fear or shame.

The silence stretched between them again, but it was a comfortable silence this time. It wasn't filled with anxiety or the unsaid words of a relationship teetering on the edge. Instead, it was filled with understanding. They were in a place of healing, and it felt right.

Leila shifted again, pulling her knees to her chest. "I guess I've been thinking about a lot of things lately," she said, her voice quieter now. "Not just about us, but about everything. School, the future, my family... Sometimes it feels like everything's just moving so fast. Like I'm running to catch up."

Destiny looked at her, her expression thoughtful. "Yeah, I get that. It's like one day everything is fine, and the next, you're trying to figure out how to deal with the mess you made."

Leila smiled, but there was a hint of sadness in her eyes. "I don't even know what I'm doing half the time. It feels like everyone else has it figured out, and I'm just... here, trying to find my place in all of it."

Destiny reached out, placing her hand over Leila's. "Hey, you're not alone in that. I feel the same way sometimes. We're both just trying to get through this crazy thing called life, and no one has it completely figured out. We're all just doing our best."

Leila gave a small, grateful nod, grateful for the words, even though they didn't completely ease the weight in her chest. She had always felt like she had to be strong like she had to be the one with all the answers. But hearing Destiny's words—knowing that

Destiny, too, was feeling uncertain—made her realize that it was okay to be lost sometimes. It was okay not to have everything together.

"We'll figure it out," Destiny added softly, her hand still resting on Leila's. "We've been through enough already. We'll make it through this too. Together."

A sense of calm settled over Leila at the words, a sense of peace she hadn't felt in a while. They'd gotten past the rough patches before, and they could do it again. This time, it would be different. They would learn from the mistakes they'd made and grow stronger because of them.

As the last rays of sunlight disappeared behind the trees, Leila sighed contentedly, feeling the tension in her body slowly dissolve. She was no longer afraid of the unknown future. With Destiny by her side, she felt like she could face whatever came her way. Maybe they didn't have all the answers. Maybe the road ahead was still filled with uncertainty. But they had each other. And that, for now, was enough.

"So, what now?" Leila asked after a few moments, her voice light.

Destiny grinned, her eyes twinkling with mischief. "Well, now that we're all deep and philosophical, how about we get ice cream? I think we've earned it."

Leila laughed, the sound was easy and genuine. "That sounds perfect."

They stood together, brushing the grass off their jeans, and started walking toward the park exit. It was a simple moment, but for Leila, it felt like a fresh start. The future was still uncertain, but for the first time in a long time, it didn't feel as overwhelming. She had a friend who understood her, and who was there through the highs and lows. And that was more than enough.

As they walked side by side, the world around them seemed to fade away, leaving just the two of them. It wasn't a perfect world, but it was theirs, and that was all that mattered.

As they strolled out of the park, Leila couldn't help but feel a sense of relief wash over her. She had spent so long trying to carry the weight of everything on her own, but at this moment, she realized that the burden felt lighter with Destiny by her side. The conversation hadn't fixed everything, but it had taken the first step toward healing—something she hadn't thought was possible just a few days ago.

"I still can't believe we're talking about this," Leila said, glancing over at Destiny with a small smile. "I never thought we'd get here."

"I know," Destiny replied, her voice light. "It felt like we were stuck in this weird loop of misunderstandings and unspoken words. But now it's like... we've broken through it. I think we both needed this more than we realized."

Leila nodded. "Yeah. I guess sometimes you don't know how much you need something until you finally do it."

They walked in comfortable silence for a few moments, both of them lost in their thoughts. The evening air had cooled, and the streetlights began flickering on, casting long shadows on the sidewalk. The world around them seemed to slow down as if it were giving them a moment to breathe before the next chapter of their lives began.

"So, what now?" Destiny asked, breaking the silence. "I mean, now that we've had our deep talk... where do we go from here?"

Leila's first instinct was to answer with something light, something that would keep the mood up, but instead, she paused. She'd been thinking about that very question all afternoon— where did they go from here? It wasn't just about mending their friendship anymore. It was about everything else: high school, their futures, what came after graduation. It was a lot to handle for anyone, but the thought of navigating it with Destiny by her side made the unknown seem a little more manageable.

"I don't know," Leila admitted, her voice soft. "I guess we take it one step at a time. Maybe we need to start talking more... like really talking. Not just about the big stuff, but the little things too. The stuff we don't usually say."

Destiny smiled, her eyes gleaming with understanding. "Yeah. I like that idea. We've kept so many things bottled up over the years, haven't we? It's time we change that."

Leila felt a surge of gratitude toward her friend. She had always known Destiny was someone she could count on, but today had proven it in a way that went beyond what she had ever imagined. It wasn't just about being there for each other when things were easy; it was about having the strength to stay through the hard parts too.

"So, ice cream?" Destiny asked, nudging her with her elbow, a playful grin on her face.

Leila chuckled. "I'm starting to think you just want an excuse to get sugar."

"Maybe," Destiny said with a wink. "But hey, I think we've earned it. We've survived the emotional rollercoaster of our conversation. We need a reward."

Leila laughed, a real laugh this time, the kind that made her feel lighter inside. "Alright, alright. You win. Ice cream it is."

The two of them made their way toward the local ice cream shop, and as they walked through the streets, the city felt different. Less daunting. They had shared a moment of honesty, one that had not only mended the cracks in their friendship but had also brought them closer in a way neither of them had expected.

As they entered the small shop, the familiar smell of waffle cones and chocolate greeted them, and Leila felt a small sense of comfort. She had been coming to this place for years, but tonight it felt different. More significant. She wasn't just getting ice cream with a friend; she was beginning a new chapter of their friendship, one built on openness and trust.

"What are you getting?" Destiny asked, peering over the counter at the colorful selection of flavors.

"Something chocolate," Leila replied automatically. "You?"

"Hmm, probably cookies and cream. Classic."

Leila grinned. "I should've known."

They ordered their ice creams and sat down at a small booth by the window, their spoons scraping the sides of the cups as they dug in. The shop was quiet, save for the soft hum of conversation and the occasional jingle of the door opening as people came in for their sweet treats. It felt like the world had slowed down for them, just for a little while.

"So," Destiny said after a few moments of silence, her voice more thoughtful now. "What's next for us? I mean, we've talked about high school stuff, and what's going on right now. But what about the future? Are we really going to do this whole college thing, or... what do we want to do after graduation?"

Leila chewed on her ice cream, her mind turning over the question. It wasn't an easy one. The future always felt so big, so overwhelming. But now, with the sense of peace between them, she felt like she could face it.

"I think we're both going to have to figure it out as we go," Leila said slowly, looking over at Destiny. "But maybe that's okay. We don't need to have it all figured out now. We're still so young, and we've got time. We've got each other, and that's enough for me."

Destiny smiled a soft, contented smile that made Leila's heart feel light. "Yeah. I think you're right. As long as we're in it together, we'll make it work."

Chapter 4
Shifting Ground

The sun had barely risen when Leila's phone buzzed on the nightstand, its persistent vibrations dragging her from the depths of sleep. She groaned, rolling over to swipe at the screen, her blurry vision slowly adjusting to the brightness. It was too early for this. She didn't even need to check the time to know that, but when she did, she saw it was barely 7 AM. A Saturday.

Her eyes narrowed in frustration, then softened when she saw the name on the screen: Destiny.

"Hey," she answered, trying to clear the grogginess from her voice. "What's up?"

"Leila, wake up! You're not gonna believe what just happened," Destiny's voice crackled through the phone, her excitement unmistakable even through the sleepiness.

Leila sat up, rubbing her eyes. "What? What's going on?"

"I think I've figured it out!" Destiny continued, breathless. "I think I know what I want to do after graduation."

Leila blinked, still processing the earlier words. "Wait, really? After all this time of not knowing?"

"Yep!" Destiny's voice was practically buzzing with energy.

"I've been doing some thinking, and I've finally decided. I want to go to art school. I've always been passionate about it, but I was too scared to admit it."

Leila's heart skipped a beat. She could feel her friend's nervousness through the phone, even though the words were full of excitement. She had known Destiny was talented when it came to painting, sketching, and photography, but the idea of art school had always felt like a distant dream.

"Art school?" Leila echoed, still trying to process the sudden news. "Destiny, that's amazing! I mean, I always knew you had it in you. But you've been so focused on... well, everything else, you know?"

"I know, I know," Destiny sighed, her voice softening. "It's just that I've always been worried about what people would think. It's not exactly a practical career choice, right? Everyone expects me to go to a regular college, do something with a degree that's more... well, stable."

Leila's heart clenched at that. She had heard Destiny's doubts before, but to hear them out loud again stung. "I don't care what anyone else thinks, Destiny. If this is what you want to do, then you should do it. You've always been so creative, and I know it would make you happy."

There was a long pause before Destiny spoke again, her voice quieter now. "You really think I can do it?"

Leila smiled, even though Destiny couldn't see it. "Of course, I do. You've got the talent, the drive... I mean, look at everything you've already done. I've seen your work, Destiny. You're already doing it."

"I guess... but what about us? What about everything else?" Destiny's voice faltered. "What if it means we won't see each other much? What if it's not the right choice after all?"

Leila felt a pang of concern, but she knew Destiny needed her reassurance now more than ever. "We're always gonna be friends, Destiny. No matter what happens after graduation. We're gonna figure it out together, even if we're going in different directions."

There was a brief silence, and then Destiny exhaled a breath of relief. "You're right. You're totally right. I just needed to hear you say it."

"Anytime," Leila replied, her voice firm with certainty. "And you're going to crush it, Destiny. Don't let anyone or anything hold you back."

Destiny laughed softly. "Thanks, Leila. You always know how to put my mind at ease."

Leila's heart swelled with pride for her friend. "That's what friends are for."

"Alright, well... I've gotta go tell my parents now," Destiny said, her voice suddenly turning anxious. "Wish me luck."

"Good luck!" Leila said, a grin spreading across her face. "I know they'll be proud of you."

"Thanks again, Leila," Destiny said before hanging up.

Leila stared at her phone for a few moments, her thoughts swirling. She couldn't believe how much had changed in just a few weeks. It felt like she and Destiny had gone through an emotional rollercoaster, but somehow, they were both coming out of it stronger. The bond they had forged during their hard conversations had solidified, and now, it was clear that they both had their own paths to follow.

But even though Destiny's decision to pursue art school filled Leila with pride, it also made her feel a sense of uncertainty. Her own future, once so clear, now seemed distant and foggy. She had been so focused on helping Destiny that she hadn't really given much thought to what came after high school for herself.

Sighing, Leila tossed her phone aside and flopped back onto her bed. Her mind was racing with questions. What did she want? What was her next step? All she had ever really been sure of was the fact that she wanted to make a difference in the world—help people in some way, maybe even make a lasting impact.

But how? And in what way?

The possibilities felt overwhelming. She thought about her family's expectations—her mom had always wanted her to go into business, to take over the family's small but successful café. Leila had always pushed back against that idea, knowing deep down that she wanted something more, something meaningful. But what if she disappointed them? What if she failed?

Her phone buzzed again, and this time it was a text from her mom: *Leila, don't forget we have dinner with your aunt and uncle tonight! Be ready by 6!*

A wave of dread washed over her. Dinner with family always seemed to be a reminder of the things she hadn't accomplished, the things they thought she should. But maybe, just maybe, she could use tonight to figure out her own path. If anything, she needed to start trusting herself a little more.

Leila grabbed her phone, typing a quick response to her mom: *Got it. I'll be ready.*

But as she put the phone down and stood to get ready for the day, she couldn't shake the feeling that everything was about to change. Destiny had taken the first step toward following her dreams, and Leila knew that she needed to take her own leap too. It wasn't going to be easy, but she was ready.

Leila stared at her reflection in the mirror, adjusting the collar of her jacket for the third time. The evening dinner with her aunt and uncle loomed ahead, and with it, a thousand questions and unspoken expectations that she couldn't shake. She had long ago stopped feeling like she could meet all of them, yet somehow, they still found a way to linger, to creep up every time she had to face her family.

Her mom's voice echoed in her mind, reminding her of the dreams she had once been told were within reach. Get good grades. Go to college. Do something with a future. The road had always been laid out for her, and the farther she walked, the clearer it became that it was a path she wasn't sure she wanted to take anymore.

With a final sigh, she grabbed her bag and left her room, the weight of indecision still hanging over her. As she stepped into the living room, she found her mom already preparing a platter of roasted vegetables, humming to herself as the scent of garlic and rosemary filled the air. Her dad, always the quiet one, sat at the kitchen table with his laptop open, working as he often did before the family gathered for their meal.

"Leila, you look great! Are you excited for dinner?" her mom asked, glancing up from her preparations with a smile.

Leila forced a smile, nodding, but inside, she was anything but excited. "Yeah, sure," she said. "Just... not really in the mood to talk about the future, if you know what I mean."

Her mom's expression shifted, but it wasn't a surprise. She had known the conversation was coming, and yet, she had hoped Leila would eventually get past her rebellious phase.

"Oh, sweetie, come on," her mom said with a sigh. "It's just a dinner. You've always been so serious about your future, but you can't let it weigh you down forever. Let's just enjoy tonight. Talk to your uncle and aunt, they'll help you see the bigger picture."

Leila didn't want to think about the "bigger picture" right now. The bigger picture had been laid out for her since she was old enough to hold a pencil. It had always been about succeeding and checking the boxes. Go to college. Become successful. Build a stable life.

But where did that leave her? Where did she fit into all of it?

As if reading her mind, her dad spoke up from the table without looking up. "You know, Leila, you don't have to have everything figured out right now."

She looked at him in surprise. Her dad didn't usually speak much during these kinds of dinners, preferring to let her mom handle the conversations. He had always been the silent observer, nodding approvingly at whatever her mom said. But now, his voice sounded different, more open.

"Yeah, you're right," she muttered, feeling the stirrings of a connection she hadn't anticipated. "But it feels like everyone else has their plans, and I'm the one still figuring it out."

Her mom shot her a glance, the subtle frustration returning to her features. "You're still young. You have time. But if you want a future, you can't waste it."

Leila bit her lip, the words stinging. She knew her mom meant well, but sometimes the pressure felt like a weight too heavy to carry. The thought of deciding her future so soon made her feel suffocated.

Before she could respond, the doorbell rang a welcome distraction. She rushed to the door and opened it to find her aunt and uncle standing there, smiling warmly, as they always did. Her aunt, tall with graying hair pulled into a neat bun, and her uncle, who always wore a serious expression despite his gentle nature.

"Leila! Look at you, all grown up," her aunt said, pulling her into a tight hug. "It feels like yesterday you were just a little thing running around the house."

Leila smiled, pulling away. "Thanks, Aunt Lucy. Good to see you."

Her uncle nodded, offering a handshake that quickly turned into a hug as well. "I hope you're doing well," he said quietly. "Your mom tells me you've been having a lot on your mind lately."

Leila wasn't surprised by the comment. Her mom loved to talk about her, even when she didn't want her to. It wasn't the first time her parents had shared something with the family that she hadn't agreed with, but she forced a smile, determined not to show how much it bothered her.

"I'm good," she said with a slight shrug. "Just trying to figure things out."

"Is that so?" her uncle asked, his tone thoughtful. "You know, I've always said that the best way to figure things out is to just follow your gut. That's how your aunt and I have made it this far. No plan, just the courage to follow where life leads."

Leila was taken aback. Her uncle had always been one to steer clear of such personal topics, preferring instead to talk about business or the weather. For him to offer her this kind of advice felt different.

She didn't know what to say at first, but before she could find the right words, her aunt jumped in, guiding everyone toward the dining room. "Well, let's not stand around talking. Dinner's getting cold, and I'm sure we've all got a lot to catch up on."

The conversation quickly turned to other matters as they sat down to eat. Leila's aunt and uncle discussed their travels, and her mom filled them in on the latest happenings at the café. Leila picked at her food, her mind still spinning from the conversation earlier, from Destiny's excitement about her future and the newfound decision to pursue art. She couldn't help but think about how much simpler things seemed for Destiny. The road was clear for her now, and while Leila was happy for her, it made her own path seem all the more uncertain.

As dinner wound down and the dessert plates were cleared away, Leila's uncle turned to her again, his eyes kind. "Leila, I don't mean to put you on the spot, but... your mom tells me you're having some doubts about your future."

She looked up, surprised by his directness but also thankful for the softness in his voice. She had always admired how her uncle never judged and never rushed people to make decisions.

"I guess I don't know what I want to do," she admitted, her voice quieter now. "I know what everyone else expects of me, but I'm not sure it's what I want."

Her aunt and uncle exchanged a glance, and her aunt smiled gently. "Leila, you don't have to have all the answers right now. Sometimes the journey to figuring it out takes time. And in the meantime, just focus on doing what feels right for you."

Leila sat back, a weight lifting from her shoulders. For the first time in what felt like forever, someone was telling her to take it slow, to breathe. She realized she didn't have to figure it all out tonight, or even in the next few months. She had time. And she wasn't alone in this.

The evening stretched on, and the conversation flowed around her. Her aunt and uncle chatted about their recent trip to Europe, regaling the family with stories of the picturesque landscapes and charming cafes they had discovered in France and Italy. Leila listened half-heartedly, her mind still tangled in the confusion of her future.

She hadn't expected her uncle to open up to her like that. His words were simple but profound, almost like a quiet invitation to consider a different way of thinking, a way that didn't require a set path or immediate answers. Leila realized that she had been running on autopilot for so long—focused only on meeting expectations—that she hadn't taken a moment to really consider what *she* wanted, what truly sparked joy for her.

Still, the weight of the questions hung in the air. What did she actually want? She hadn't allowed herself to think beyond the rigid structure of success. Her friends seemed to have figured it out, moving forward with passion and purpose, while Leila felt like she was floundering, drifting between expectations and uncertainty.

After dessert, when the conversation had tapered off and everyone was content with their cups of tea or coffee, her aunt looked at her with a knowing smile.

"Leila, sweetheart, you're a thinker. Always have been. But sometimes, you can't think your way into clarity. Sometimes, you have to feel your way through it. And I know that's hard to understand when you're so used to logic and planning. But trust me, you'll figure it out."

Leila nodded, absorbing her aunt's words. It wasn't the kind of advice she had come here for, but it was the kind she needed. Her aunt had always had a way of cutting through the noise and offering simple truths.

"Maybe I just need to... relax a bit," Leila said, almost to herself.

Her uncle leaned forward, his voice quieter now. "Leila, the truth is, you don't have to follow someone else's map. Build your own, even if it takes you down a winding road. You're young, and you've got time. But don't waste it trying to fit into a mold that's not yours."

The weight that had settled on her chest seemed to lighten ever so slightly. Leila glanced at her mom, who had been quiet for a while now. Her mother had a distant look in her eyes like she was lost in thought. Leila knew her mom well enough to recognize that look; it was the same one her mom wore whenever she felt uncertain or conflicted.

Finally, after what felt like an eternity, her mom spoke. "Leila, I know I've been pushing you to think about your future, and I don't want you to think that I don't believe in you. It's just... I want you to succeed. I want you to have the kind of life I've always dreamed for you."

Her voice trailed off, and for a moment, the weight of her mother's unspoken worries hung in the air. Leila knew it came from a place of love, but the pressure was suffocating at times.

"I know, Mom. I know you want what's best for me," Leila said softly. "But sometimes, I need to figure that out on my own. I just need some space."

Her mother met her gaze, her lips pressing together in a thin line as she processed Leila's words. There was a long pause before her mom sighed, a reluctant but understanding gesture.

"I understand," she said. "I just don't want you to make the same mistakes I did. I wish I had taken more risks when I was your age."

Leila blinked, surprised by the vulnerability in her mother's voice. She had never heard her mom talk about her own regrets before. It made Leila feel both sad and strangely comforted, as if there was a shared understanding now, a bridge between them that had not existed before.

"Maybe I'll start taking a few more risks," Leila said, her voice firmer now, the idea starting to take root. She wasn't sure what that would look like, but the thought felt like a small step toward freedom.

Her mom smiled, albeit a little sadly, and nodded. "I hope you do, sweetie. I really do."

The evening wound down, and after saying their goodbyes, Leila and her family cleaned up. As the night deepened, the house felt quieter, as if the conversations that had taken place had lifted something off everyone's shoulders. Leila stood by the sink, washing the last of the dishes, her thoughts wandering.

She could feel the shift inside her, a quiet kind of change. She didn't have all the answers, but maybe, for the first time in a while, she didn't need to have them right away. The uncertainty was still there, lingering like an unfinished sentence, but Leila was beginning to realize that it didn't have to be a source of dread.

As she put the final dish in the drying rack, her phone buzzed on the counter. She wiped her hands quickly and picked it up, seeing a text from Destiny.

Destiny: Hey, I know we've been kind of off lately, but I've been thinking about you. How are you doing?

Leila felt a small smile tug at her lips. She hadn't talked to Destiny in days. Things had been strained ever since their disagreement about college and the direction their lives were heading. But maybe this was the first step toward mending things.

Leila: I'm good. Actually, I think I'm figuring a few things out. I don't have all the answers, but I'm starting to think it's okay not to have everything figured out.

She paused before hitting send, wondering if Destiny would understand what she meant. But the text felt right.

Destiny: That's good to hear. I've been thinking a lot about things too. Maybe we can talk soon?

Leila's heart warmed at the thought. A part of her had been afraid that their friendship might be slipping away, but maybe it wasn't too late to reconnect, to rebuild what they had.

Leila: I'd like that. Let's hang out soon.

She hit send, then placed her phone back down, her mind swirling with possibilities. For the first time in a long while, she felt a sense of calm settle over her. She wasn't in control of everything, and maybe that was okay. The pieces were starting to fall into place, even if they weren't in the exact shape she had expected.

The next few days passed in a blur of activity. Leila's world felt like it was gently spinning, a calm undercurrent running beneath the surface as she processed the new thoughts and ideas that had started to take root in her mind. The conversations with her aunt and uncle had done something unexpected—something subtle but powerful. She felt like she had a little more space to breathe, to think outside the rigid walls of expectation she had built around herself.

At school, things felt different. As the week progressed, Leila found herself lost in thought more often than usual. She would walk down the hallways, her mind churning with possibilities. The pressure to have everything figured out still loomed large, but it no longer felt as suffocating. She realized she wasn't alone in this struggle. Everyone around her seemed to be navigating their own tangled paths, just like she was. The only difference was that they were, at least, out loud about their doubts.

During lunch on Friday, Destiny found her at their usual spot in the cafeteria. She slid into the seat next to Leila with a grin, and Leila felt a rush of warmth at the sight of her friend.

"I was beginning to think you'd forgotten about me," Destiny teased, but there was a softness to her voice that Leila recognized immediately.

"Not a chance," Leila replied, nudging her playfully. "I've just been... thinking, I guess."

Destiny raised an eyebrow, clearly intrigued. "Thinking? About what?"

Leila hesitated for a moment before she spoke. She wasn't sure how much she wanted to reveal yet, but something in Destiny's open expression made her feel like it was the right time to share.

"About the future, I guess," Leila said slowly. "And how I don't need to have it all figured out. I mean, you know how much pressure I've been feeling lately, right? I've been so focused on following the plan that I've never really thought about what *I* want."

Destiny nodded. "Yeah, I get that. It's like we're all expected to have our futures mapped out, like right now. But I don't know if that's even realistic. Not for me, anyway."

Leila felt a flood of relief wash over her at Destiny's words. It was nice to hear someone else voice what she had been quietly grappling with for so long. "Exactly! I've been thinking... I don't need to follow someone else's plan. I can make my own, even if it doesn't look like everyone else's."

Destiny smiled widely, her eyes sparkling with understanding. "That's exactly what I've been trying to say! Who decided that the 'right' way is the only way? I think we're both allowed to carve out our own paths, even if they look completely different from each other."

Leila nodded enthusiastically, her heart lighter than it had been in a long time. She hadn't realized just how much she needed to hear those words from someone who understood.

"But, what if we mess up?" Leila asked, a flicker of doubt creeping into her mind. "What if we make the wrong choice and regret it later?"

Destiny's expression softened. "You know, I think the fear of regret holds a lot of people back. We're afraid of making mistakes, but... mistakes aren't the end of the world. They're how we learn. I think you'll figure it out. I know I will."

Leila looked at her friend, feeling a swell of gratitude. Destiny had always been the one to say what needed to be said, to help her see things from a different angle.

"You're right," Leila said, her voice quiet but sure. "Maybe we're not supposed to have everything figured out all at once."

Destiny nodded, and for a moment, they both just sat there, lost in their own thoughts. The world seemed to fall away, and for the first time in a while, Leila felt like she was on the right track—not toward certainty, but toward something real and true.

As lunch ended and the bell rang, signaling the return to class, Leila felt lighter than she had in days. The conversation with Destiny had been exactly what she needed—a reminder that it was okay not to have all the answers, that she could take things one step at a time.

The next week, Leila took the first real step toward living in alignment with herself. She signed up for a volunteer position at a local community center, helping with after-school programs for younger kids. It wasn't the glamorous, high-status job that her parents had envisioned for her, but it felt right. She was excited about it—excited to work with the kids and to learn from them. It was a way to give back, yes, but also to explore a different side of herself, one that she had never allowed to emerge before.

Her parents were... less than thrilled, but they were supportive. Leila could sense that they still had doubts, and still believed she should be doing something more "important," but for the first time, their opinions didn't have the same hold over her.

That Friday, after the first day at the community center, Leila met Destiny at their usual spot by the lockers. Destiny's face lit up when she saw her.

"How was it?" she asked, her voice filled with curiosity.

"It was... amazing," Leila said, her face glowing with excitement. "The kids were so sweet, and they're full of energy. I didn't think I'd have this much fun. It's definitely not what I thought I'd be doing, but I think I'm exactly where I'm supposed to be."

Destiny smiled, clearly proud of her friend. "I'm so happy for you, Leila. It sounds like you're really finding your path. This is just the beginning, isn't it?"

Leila nodded, her heart full. "Yeah. It feels like it."

And for the first time in a long time, Leila was no longer afraid of the unknown. She knew the road ahead might be difficult, that there would be bumps along the way, but for the first time, she was ready to face it all on her own terms.

The next few weeks passed in a blur of personal growth and newfound realizations. Leila had thrown herself into her volunteer work, and with each day, she discovered more about herself than she ever thought possible. The community center felt like a home away from home. The kids' laughter, their curiosity, and their boundless energy slowly started to break down the walls Leila had put up around her heart.

Her relationship with her parents, however, remained strained. They didn't fully understand her decision to focus on this volunteer work, and while they didn't outright oppose it, their subtle disapproval hung in the air like an unspoken tension. Her mother would occasionally suggest, in that way, mothers do, that Leila should consider a "backup plan," just in case. Leila had learned to nod and smile, knowing that their intentions were rooted in love, but also knowing that their vision for her life was no longer the one she wanted to pursue.

At school, things were still a mixed bag. Leila had yet to figure out the complexities of teenage friendships, especially with someone as unpredictable as Destiny. Their connection was undeniable, yet still fragile in some ways. Destiny was fiercely loyal, but sometimes her bluntness left Leila questioning whether their differences were more than just surface-level. It wasn't easy to keep up with Destiny's energy and spontaneity, but Leila found herself wanting to try. After all, she was learning to embrace change, and maybe that included embracing parts of herself that she'd ignored in the past.

One afternoon, as Leila was sitting on the bleachers at the community center watching the kids run around outside, Destiny joined her, plopping down beside her with a grin.

"Hey, Leila," she said, stretching her legs out in front of her. "I've got a crazy idea. What do you think about hitting the town this weekend? Just the two of us. No plans. Just... whatever happens."

Leila glanced at Destiny, intrigued but cautious. "You know, we've never done anything like that. It sounds fun, but—"

"Exactly," Destiny interrupted with a mischievous glint in her eyes. "That's why it'll be great! We don't have to think about anything, just... be in the moment. Besides, you deserve to have a little fun, right? You've been working hard. I think you've earned a bit of chaos."

Leila laughed despite herself, the idea appealing more than she'd care to admit. The truth was, part of her had been craving a break, a moment to let loose and forget the weight of expectations. She wasn't used to stepping outside the lines, but that was starting to feel like the whole point of this new chapter in her life.

"Alright, let's do it," she said, a wide grin spreading across her face.

Destiny's eyes lit up, and for the rest of the afternoon, Leila found herself in a daze, imagining the possibilities of a day spent without any rules. It had been a while since she'd let herself think like that.

That weekend, they did exactly what Destiny had suggested— no plans, just wandering. They started by getting coffee at a small shop on the corner of a street neither of them had explored before. The place was quirky, with mismatched furniture and abstract art on the walls. It felt like a secret spot, just for them. They laughed over ridiculous lattes with too much-whipped cream and talked about everything and nothing all at once.

Leila was surprised by how comfortable she felt. There was a warmth in the air that day, and for the first time in a while, she didn't feel like she had to pretend. There were no expectations of her, no future plans to obsess over.

After coffee, they wandered the town, exploring every nook and cranny. They stumbled into a bookstore, one that smelled of old pages and quiet secrets. Leila ran her fingers along the spines of books, savoring the sensation. They found a small café by a park and sat in the sunshine, their feet up on the bench, feeling carefree.

It was all so simple, and yet, for Leila, it was the first time in months that she felt truly alive.

Later that night, as they sat on the grass near the water, watching the last colors of the sunset fade into dusk, Destiny turned to her, her expression serious for once.

"You know, Leila," she began, her voice soft, "I'm really proud of you. I know things haven't been easy, and I know you're still figuring things out. But I can see that you're growing. I can see it in the way you talk about what you want. You're not the same person you were when I first met you."

Leila felt a lump rise in her throat, emotions she hadn't fully realized were building up inside of her. She hadn't realized how much she needed to hear those words, how much it meant to have someone truly see her.

"I'm just... trying," Leila said, her voice quiet. "I don't know if I'll ever have it all figured out, but I'm learning that maybe that's okay. And maybe... maybe I don't have to be perfect. I can just be me."

Destiny smiled, the sincerity in her eyes making Leila's heart swell. "Exactly. Just be you. And know that I'm here, no matter what."

They sat there in silence for a while, the weight of those words settling between them like a quiet promise. Leila had never felt so understood. Maybe it had taken her a little longer to get there, but she finally felt like she was on the right path. It wasn't about having all the answers. It was about embracing the questions and trusting that, with time, she would find her way.

The weekend ended all too quickly, but Leila felt lighter, and more at peace with herself than she had in a long time. It was a small, fleeting moment of freedom, but it was enough. For the first time in ages, she felt like she could breathe.

As the days turned into weeks, Leila continued her volunteer work at the community center, finding new purpose in every smile she encountered. The path ahead was still uncertain, but she no longer felt so afraid of it. And with Destiny by her side, supporting her every step of the way, Leila was ready to face whatever challenges the future held.

As the week wore on, the bond between Leila and Destiny grew in ways neither of them expected. After their spontaneous day out, they seemed to understand each other more than ever. It wasn't just the shared moments of laughter and unspoken camaraderie that brought them closer; it was the unguarded conversations and the honest vulnerability that came with letting go of expectations. Leila had always admired Destiny's ability to live in the moment, to embrace uncertainty without fear, but now, she was starting to understand how liberating it could be.

But as much as their friendship was deepening, there was still an undeniable tension at home. Leila's parents, particularly her mother, remained skeptical of her newfound path. They didn't fully understand why she was prioritizing her work at the community center over the academic goals they had set for her. Leila often found herself retreating into the comfort of her own thoughts, navigating this inner conflict about the life she was building versus the one they envisioned for her.

One evening, after a long shift at the community center, Leila was sitting at the kitchen table, sipping on her tea. Her parents were at the other end of the room, talking quietly about the day's events. The hum of the conversation wasn't unfamiliar, but tonight, something felt different. Her mother glanced over at her, catching her gaze for a moment before looking away.

"Leila, how was your day?" her father asked, his tone casual, but his eyes watching her intently.

"It was fine," Leila answered, not wanting to get into the intricacies of her volunteer work and how much it meant to her. She knew they didn't see the value in it.

"Are you sure that's all? You've been quiet lately," her mother added, concern laced in her voice. "You know, you really should be focused on your grades. It's one thing to be helping out, but what about your future?"

Leila's heart sank as the familiar tension built in her chest. Her mother's words stung, as they always did. It wasn't that she didn't care about her future; it was just that she wanted a different kind of future than the one they had imagined for her.

"I'm doing my best, Mom," she said softly, her fingers tracing the edge of her teacup. "But... I'm not sure what the future looks like. And right now, I'm finding fulfillment in other things."

Her father shifted in his seat, and for a brief moment, there was silence between them, a kind of unspoken disconnect. It wasn't that they didn't love her. It was that they loved her in the way they thought was best, not in the way she needed.

"I just want you to be happy, Leila," her mother said after a long pause, her voice softening. "But I also want you to be practical. The world doesn't always reward idealism."

Leila's mind raced. She didn't know how to explain to them that the life she was crafting wasn't about being idealistic; it was about being real. Real with herself. Real with the people she was helping. But instead, she just nodded, feeling the weight of their expectations pressing down on her.

The conversation ended without resolution, and Leila retreated to her room, the familiar sense of isolation settling over her. For a moment, she wondered if she was making a mistake, if she was letting the things she cared about slip through her fingers for the sake of a dream that wasn't fully formed. But then she thought of the kids at the community center—their wide eyes, their thirst for learning, the way they trusted her. She couldn't just walk away from that.

The next day, Destiny came to the community center to visit her during her shift, and Leila was grateful for the distraction. Destiny had this way of bringing light into any room she entered, and today was no different. She greeted Leila with a wide grin, her energy infectious. They sat on the steps outside the building for a while, talking about everything and nothing, just letting the conversation flow.

"You know," Destiny said after a few minutes of casual chatter, "I was thinking about what you said the other night. About being real with yourself. And I think... I think you're onto something."

Leila raised an eyebrow. "Oh?"

"Yeah, you've always been this kind of quiet, thoughtful person, right? And I don't think you're hiding it or anything. You just... you don't always know how to make it fit into this world that's telling you to be loud, to stand out, to have a plan." Destiny paused, her expression thoughtful. "But the way I see it, you're doing something pretty incredible. You're helping these kids in a way that matters. And that's more than a lot of people can say for themselves."

Leila felt her heart swell at Destiny's words. It wasn't the first time Destiny had said something supportive, but it felt different now. It felt like Destiny truly understood her, and saw the parts of her that she had kept hidden for so long.

"I don't know if it's enough," Leila admitted, her voice barely above a whisper. "I mean, I love what I'm doing, but sometimes I wonder if I'm just... avoiding the real world. The future. The stuff I'm supposed to be doing."

Destiny shook her head, her smile warm and reassuring. "No, I don't think you're avoiding anything. I think you're finding your way, one step at a time. And honestly? I think that's pretty brave."

For the first time in weeks, Leila felt like she could breathe. It wasn't that she had all the answers. She still didn't know exactly what her future would look like. But for once, she didn't feel so alone in the process of figuring it out. With Destiny by her side, maybe it didn't matter if the answers came immediately or not.

As the days went by, the weight of her family's expectations began to feel a little lighter. Leila started to embrace the idea that she didn't have to have everything figured out. She didn't have to be perfect. She just had to be true to herself—and that was enough.

At the community center, the kids continued to thrive under her guidance. They looked up to her in ways that made her heart swell with pride. She might not have had all the answers, but seeing their bright smiles and eager faces reminded her that she was doing something right. And for now, that was all she needed.

Leila had no idea what the future held, but she knew one thing for sure: she wasn't going to let go of the person she was becoming—not for anyone, not even for her parents. She was learning to embrace the messy, uncertain parts of life, and she was starting to realize that maybe that was the only way to truly live.

Chapter 5
The Burden of Expectations

The days seemed to blur together as Leila navigated through the complexities of her life. Her friendships, her family's expectations, and the constant undercurrent of doubt she often felt were beginning to settle into a routine. But routine, sherealized, wasn't necessarily the same thing as peace. It felt like she was walking on a tightrope—trying to balance between her desires and the demands of those around her.

The school had been demanding in its own right, but the additional weight of keeping up with the community center and managing the delicate threads of her relationships with her family was proving to be overwhelming. Each day brought a new challenge, a new conversation where she had to explain herself, to justify her choices, even though she knew deep down that these were the decisions that felt right to her.

Leila walked into the living room on a Friday afternoon, the familiar hum of the TV filling the space as her mother and father sat in their usual spots, speaking in low voices. The air was thick with the unspoken tension that always seemed to follow them when they were talking about her future. She had tried to avoid these conversations, but it was becoming impossible to ignore.

"Leila," her mother called out, her voice tinged with a mix of frustration and concern. "We need to talk."

Leila paused, hesitating for a moment before walking over to the couch. She sat down, setting her bag on the floor, feeling the weight of her mother's gaze on her.

"I know you're busy with the community center," her father started, his tone calmer than her mother's but still filled with an underlying sense of urgency. "But your grades are slipping. You're not putting enough focus on your schoolwork. We've always taught you that education comes first, Leila."

Leila felt a familiar knot form in her stomach. She had been expecting this, but it didn't make it any easier to hear. "I'm doing my best," she replied, her voice steady, though she felt the frustration rising within her. "But I can't ignore the things that matter to me. The kids at the community center—they depend on me. I'm making a difference there."

Her mother's expression softened, but there was still a trace of disbelief in her eyes. "I understand that you want to help, but your future is important, too. You can't keep putting everything else ahead of your success."

Leila bit her lip, trying to keep her emotions in check. She knew her parents meant well, but their constant pressure was beginning to suffocate her. "I'm not ignoring my future," she said quietly. "But I can't just forget the people who need me right now."

Her father sighed, looking at her with a mixture of concern and frustration. "Leila, we're not saying you shouldn't help people. We just don't want you to lose sight of what's truly important."

"I know what's important to me," she said, standing up quickly. "I don't need you to tell me. I'm figuring it out on my own."

She turned and left the room before they could respond, her heart pounding in her chest. She couldn't do this anymore. The weight of their expectations was pushing her to the edge, and she didn't know how much longer she could keep up the facade that everything was fine.

Her phone buzzed in her pocket, and she pulled it out, seeing a message from Destiny.

Destiny: Hey, are you free tonight? I thought we could go grab some dinner and talk about stuff.

Leila smiled, the tension in her chest easing just a little. Destiny was always there when she needed her, a constant source of support. She quickly typed a response.

Leila: Yeah, that sounds perfect. I'll meet you at the usual spot in an hour.

Destiny: You got it! See you soon!

Leila took a deep breath, trying to calm her nerves. She grabbed her jacket and headed out the door, eager to escape the suffocating atmosphere of her house and spend time with someone who understood her.

When Leila arrived at their usual diner, Destiny was already sitting at their favorite booth, her back turned as she scrolled through her phone. She looked up when she heard Leila approach and flashed a bright smile.

"There you are!" Destiny exclaimed. "I was getting worried you wouldn't show up."

Leila slid into the booth across from her, feeling the warmth of Destiny's presence seep into her. "Sorry, I had to get away from my parents for a bit," she said, her voice tinged with exhaustion. "They keep pressuring me to do things I'm not ready for. It's like they don't even see me anymore."

Destiny's expression softened, and she leaned forward slightly. "I know it's tough. But you're doing what feels right for you, right? That's what matters most."

Leila nodded, grateful for her friend's unwavering support. "I just don't know how much longer I can keep doing this. Every time I take a step forward, they just pull me back."

"You know," Destiny began, taking a sip of her drink, "I think you need to stop trying to make them see your path and just focus on walking it. They might never fully understand what you're doing, but that doesn't mean it's not important."

Leila felt a sense of clarity wash over her at Destiny's words.

She had been so focused on trying to gain her parents' approval that she had lost sight of the fact that she was already doing something worthwhile. She didn't need their validation to know that the work she was doing at the community center was valuable. She didn't need their permission to keep moving forward.

"You're right," Leila said, a small smile forming on her lips. "I've been letting them dictate my happiness for too long. It's time I start living for me."

Destiny grinned, her eyes sparkling with pride. "That's the Leila I know."

They spent the rest of the evening talking about everything and nothing, the conversation flowing easily as it always did. It was a rare moment of peace in the whirlwind of Leila's life, and she savored every second of it.

By the time they finished their meal and walked out into the cool night air, Leila felt lighter, as if a weight had been liftedfrom her shoulders. For the first time in a long while, she wasn't worried about what others thought of her. She was ready to move forward, to find her way, no matter what anyone else said.

As they hugged goodbye, Destiny gave her one last piece of advice. "Just remember Leila: You don't owe anyone an explanation for your happiness. You get to define it."

Leila smiled, feeling her heart swell with gratitude. "Thanks, Destiny. I needed that."

As she walked home under the starry sky, Leila felt like she had taken the first step toward something new—something that was entirely her own. The road ahead was still uncertain, but for the first time in a long time, she felt ready to face whatever came next.

Leila woke up the next morning feeling a rare sense of clarity. The conversations from the night before had settled in her mind, and for the first time in a while, she felt like she could breathe. Destiny's words echoed in her ears as she stepped out of bed and into the quiet morning. She didn't owe anyone an explanation for her happiness. It was a simple truth, but one she had been overlooking for too long.

The sun was just beginning to rise, casting a warm, golden light through her bedroom window. She stood by the window for a moment, watching the sky shift from purple to pink to soft blue. The world outside felt peaceful, and still, and for a moment, it felt like the possibilities were endless.

But as Leila began to get ready for the day, the familiar tension from yesterday crept back into her thoughts. She could already feel the pull of her parent's expectations, the looming pressure to succeed in ways that aligned with their vision of success. Even though she had decided to live for herself, the weight of their hopes wasn't something that could be shaken off so easily.

As she pulled on her jeans and a comfortable t-shirt, she glanced at her phone. The notifications were mostly school-related, but there was one message that stood out: a new reminder from the community center. Her heart quickened as she read it.

Community Center Update: Volunteer Meeting Today at 3 p.m. Please be there.

Her mind raced. She'd been working so hard at the center lately, balancing her schoolwork, family, and everything else that she had barely realized how much she had taken on. The pressure was mounting, but it was a pressure that she could handle. It was the only thing that felt like it truly mattered.

She grabbed her bag and headed downstairs to grab a quick breakfast. Her mom was in the kitchen, making coffee, and for a moment, they both just stared at each other across the counter. There was an awkward silence between them, one that seemed to stretch longer than it should.

"Leila," her mother said softly, setting the coffee cup down in front of her. "We need to talk again."

Leila swallowed her frustration. She hadn't been expecting this so soon after last night. But she had made a promise to herself that she wouldn't shy away from these moments anymore. She would speak her truth, no matter how hard it might be.

"Mom, I don't know if there's anything left to say," she replied, her voice steady but firm. "I'm doing what I feel is right for me."

Her mother's gaze softened, but there was a quiet sadness in her eyes. "I just want what's best for you, Leila. I've seen you change in the past few months, and it worries me. You're putting so much energy into other people that you're forgetting about yourself."

Leila took a deep breath, trying to calm the swirling emotions inside her. "I haven't forgotten myself," she said slowly. "I'm not doing this for anyone else. The work I'm doing at the center, the way I'm helping others—it's what makes me feel like I'm doing something important. I know it's not exactly what you and Dad imagined for me, but it's what I need."

Her mother sighed, rubbing her temple as if trying to erase the concern etched into her features. "I understand that you want to help, but it's just hard to see you running around in circles. We want you to have a solid future, Leila. I don't want to see you waste your potential on things that might not lead anywhere."

Leila felt a pang in her chest at her mother's words. But she didn't back down. She had been living in the shadow of their expectations for too long. "I'm not wasting my potential, Mom. I'm growing, and I'm learning. I know this path is unconventional, but it's mine. And I need you to accept that."

There was a long pause, and Leila could see the conflict playing out in her mother's eyes. She wasn't ready to accept her choices just yet, but Leila didn't expect her to. It was going to take time.

"Alright," her mother said after a beat. "I won't push anymore. Just... please promise me you'll keep your future in mind."

Leila nodded, though she wasn't sure if she could promise that. She couldn't make any more promises that she wasn't sure she could keep. But she would try. She would do her best to balance everything, and if it meant carving out a future for herself, one that made her proud, then she would find a way.

By the time the meeting rolled around at the community center, Leila was feeling more at peace. The conversation with her mom had been difficult, but it had also been a step in the right direction. She knew that her parents might never fully understand the direction she was heading in, but at least they were starting to listen. That was a start.

As she entered the community center, she was greeted by the familiar faces of the other volunteers, and she couldn't help but smile. This place was her second home. The kids she worked with, the staff, and even the other volunteers—they were all part of the family she had chosen for herself. They made her feel seen, and they made her feel important.

"Leila!" one of the volunteers called out, waving her over. "Glad you could make it. We've got a lot to discuss today."

Leila nodded and made her way over to the group, feeling the weight of her worries begin to lift. The work she did here was fulfilling in a way that nothing else had been. And for the first time in a while, she felt like she was on the right path.

As the meeting began, the focus was on upcoming events, plans for improving the center's programs, and new ways to support the kids in their care. Leila jumped in immediately, offering suggestions and brainstorming ideas with the rest of the team. For the first time, she felt confident in her voice, knowing that her contributions were valuable.

Hours passed in a blur, and by the time the meeting was over, Leila was exhausted but content. She lingered behind to help clean up, wiping down tables and organizing supplies, savoring the quiet satisfaction of a job well done.

As she walked back home later that evening, her phone buzzed with a new message from Destiny.

Destiny: How'd it go today?

Leila smiled as she typed her response.

Leila: It went really well. I'm feeling more sure of things than I have in a while.

Destiny: That's amazing! I'm proud of you. You've got this.

Leila grinned as she put her phone away. For the first time in a long time, she truly believed she did.

The days that followed seemed to pass in a blur. Each morning felt like a new opportunity, but there was always the weight of the decisions Leila was making, hovering just below the surface. It was as though she were walking a tightrope, trying to balance the various pieces of her life. School, family, and the community center—each piece had a different level of importance, but they all seemed to pull at her in different directions.

The weekend arrived quicker than expected, and with it, the

volunteer event at the center. Leila had been looking forward to it for days, but as she got ready, her mind wandered to what she had left behind at home. The constant conversations with her mother about her future, the pressure to excel academically, and the long hours at the center—it was all starting to feel overwhelming.

After a quick breakfast, Leila slipped on her jacket and grabbed her bag. She was running a little behind, so she hurried out of the house, her thoughts still swirling from the conversations she'd had with her mom earlier in the week. They hadn't resolved everything, and Leila wasn't sure if they ever would, but she was learning to live with the discomfort. It was hard not to feel like she was letting them down.

The community center was only a few blocks away, and the walk gave her some time to clear her head. The cool morning air felt good on her skin, and the sound of leaves rustling in the breeze was oddly calming. She could feel herself relax a little, letting the worry slip away with each step.

When she arrived, Destiny was already there, helping set up for the event. She was standing next to one of the large donation boxes, arranging the items inside. When she saw Leila, she waved enthusiastically.

"Hey, you made it! I was starting to think you were going to bail on me!" Destiny teased, but there was genuine excitement in her voice.

Leila grinned and jogged over to her. "I would never bail on you. I'm just trying to keep up with everything."

Destiny raised an eyebrow, clearly noticing the hint of exhaustion in Leila's tone. "You sure you're alright? You've been running on empty lately."

Leila sighed, rubbing the back of her neck. "Yeah, just a lot going on. You know how it is."

Destiny nodded. "I get it. But remember to take care of yourself, okay? You don't have to do everything."

"I know," Leila said, but her voice lacked conviction. She couldn't help it; the weight of responsibility was heavy. "I just... I don't want to disappoint anyone, you know?"

Destiny paused for a moment, her eyes softening with understanding. "Leila, I get it. But you can't keep carrying the weight of the world on your shoulders. Sometimes, you have to let go a little. It's okay to not have it all figured out."

Leila gave a small smile. "I'll try. I just feel like I'm constantly pulled in so many directions. It's hard to keep up."

Destiny reached out and gave her shoulder a reassuring squeeze. "You're doing great. You just need to remember that you're allowed to take breaks. You're not Superwoman."

Leila chuckled. "Yeah, well, if I were Superwoman, I'd be able to keep it all together."

Destiny smiled, but there was a flicker of concern in her eyes. "Seriously though, just don't burn yourself out, okay? You matter more than anything else."

Leila nodded, feeling a warmth spread through her chest at the kindness in Destiny's words. For the first time in a while, she felt like maybe she wasn't alone in this. Her best friend understood her struggles, and it felt like a weight was being lifted, just by hearing those words.

They both turned their attention to the event, focusing on setting up. The morning passed quickly as they arranged tables, unpacked boxes of donations, and got everything ready. There was a hum of activity in the air, and Leila felt herself getting lost in the rhythm of it all. The stress of the week seemed to melt away as she interacted with the kids and helped the staff with preparations.

By the time the event kicked off, Leila felt a sense of fulfillment she hadn't experienced in a long time. Watching the kids engage in the activities, seeing their faces light up as they learned new things, made everything else seem less important. This was what mattered. This was why she kept going, despite the exhaustion, despite the pressure from home.

In the afternoon, as the event began to wind down, Leila found herself standing by the snack table, her eyes scanning the room. She caught sight of Destiny, who was talking to a group of kids nearby. Her friend seemed so at ease, as though the world was perfectly aligned around her. Leila envied that sense of calm. She wished she could feel as confident in her own choices.

But as she looked around, she realized that maybe she didn't need to have everything figured out right now. Destiny was right: it was okay to not have it all together. She could keep moving forward, step by step, without feeling like she had to know everything at once.

Just as that thought settled in her mind, a familiar voice interrupted her thoughts.

"You look deep in thought."

Leila turned to see her mother standing by the entrance, looking slightly out of place among the bustling crowd. It wasn't often that her mom came to one of these events, but here she was, watching Leila with a mixture of curiosity and concern.

"Mom?" Leila said, surprised. "What are you doing here?"

Her mother smiled gently, her eyes softening as she watched her daughter. "I wanted to see what this was all about. To see for myself what you've been doing."

Leila felt a swell of emotion in her chest. She hadn't expected her mother to show up, much less express an interest in her work at the center. But here she was, trying to understand.

"I didn't think you'd... I mean, I didn't know you cared this much," Leila admitted, her voice tinged with disbelief.

Her mother's smile grew. "I do care, Leila. Maybe I haven't been the most supportive lately, but I'm trying. I want to understand."

Leila swallowed, trying to push down the lump in her throat. "Thank you, Mom."

They stood there in silence for a moment, watching the event unfold before them. Leila wasn't sure what the future held, but in that moment, with her mother standing by her side and Destiny nearby, she felt like she was exactly where she needed to be.

As the afternoon wore on, the event began to wind down. The noise of children laughing, running around, and the soft murmur of adults chatting slowly faded. Leila watched as the final few families made their way out, their faces full of smiles and excitement from the activities they'd participated in. She felt a deep sense of pride watching the way the community had come together. But underneath that pride, there was a lingering heaviness that wouldn't let go.

Her mother had stayed through most of the event, chatting with some of the other parents and volunteers. Leila had tried to push the discomfort she felt about her mom's sudden interest in her life to the back of her mind, but she couldn't shake the feeling that something had changed. It was like a bridge had been built between them, but Leila wasn't sure whether she was ready to cross it yet.

The event ended with a round of applause from the volunteers and staff. Leila stood with Destiny, who was helping pack up the leftover supplies. The bright energy of the day was starting to fade, and Leila felt the familiar tug of exhaustion pulling at her. Destiny was still chatting away, but Leila's mind was elsewhere, lost in her thoughts.

"Are you okay?" Destiny asked, glancing over at her. "You look like you're a million miles away."

Leila blinked, coming back to reality. "Oh, yeah. Just... thinking."

"About what?" Destiny prodded, her tone gentle.

Leila paused, her eyes scanning the room as she tried to find the right words. "About everything. My mom is here... and how things are changing. It just feels like... like I don't know how to keep up with all of it."

Destiny stopped packing up the supplies and turned her full attention to Leila. "You know, you don't have to figure everything out right now. And you don't have to carry the world on your shoulders."

"I know," Leila said, her voice quiet. "But sometimes it feels like I have to."

Destiny placed a hand on her shoulder. "Leila, you're doing an amazing job. But you don't have to do it all alone. I'm here, and your mom is here now. You have people who care about you."

Leila let out a small laugh. "I just... I don't know if I'm ready to let people in, you know?"

Destiny nodded, understanding. "Yeah. I get that. It's not easy. But sometimes, letting people in isn't about letting them take over your life. It's just about having someone by your side when things get tough."

Leila smiled at her friend, feeling a wave of gratitude for the unwavering support Destiny had always given her. "Thanks, Destiny. I don't know what I'd do without you."

"You'd probably be doing a lot of stuff on your own," Destiny teased, her grin wide. "But, hey, I like to think I make things easier."

Leila chuckled, feeling lighter. "You definitely do."

As they finished packing up the last of the supplies, Leila's mother approached them. She had her coat on and a soft smile on her face. Leila's heart skipped a beat—she had no idea what to expect now that her mom was here.

"Leila," her mom began, her voice hesitant, "I just wanted to say thank you for letting me be a part of today. I know I haven't always been the best at showing up for you, but today made me realize just how important this is to you. And... I'm proud of you."

Leila froze for a moment, the words hitting her harder than she expected. Her mom was proud of her. She hadn't heard those words from her in what felt like forever. A lump formed in her throat, and for a second, she wasn't sure how to respond.

"Thanks, Mom," Leila said softly, her voice shaky. She took a breath, trying to steady herself. "I'm glad you came. I didn't expect that, but it means a lot."

Her mother smiled, her eyes warm. "I know. I'm trying to be better. And if you ever need anything... just know I'm here."

For a moment, it felt like the weight of years of tension between them was starting to lift. But Leila didn't know what to make of it. She had spent so long trying to figure things out on her own, and now, suddenly, it felt like there was this new opening between them.

"I'll keep that in mind," Leila said. "But right now, I think I need a little break from everything. It's been a long day."

Her mother nodded. "Of course. Take care of yourself, Leila. You deserve it."

Leila watched her mother walk toward the exit, and for the first time in a long while, she felt like maybe things could start to get better. Slowly. It wouldn't be an overnight change, but it was a start.

"Come on, let's get out of here," Destiny said, nudging her with an elbow. "We've earned it."

Leila smiled and followed Destiny out of the building, her mind still buzzing but her heart feeling lighter. As they stepped into the cool evening air, Leila realized that while there was still a lot of uncertainty ahead, she wasn't as alone in it as she had felt before. There were people who cared about her, people who were willing to help her navigate through the chaos.

For the first time in what felt like ages, Leila allowed herself to feel a little hopeful.

The next morning, as she prepared for another busy day, Leila decided to take Destiny's advice to heart. She didn't have to figure everything out right away. She could take it one step at a time. And maybe, just maybe, she could let herself lean on the people who wanted to be there for her.

The next day, Leila woke up to the sound of her alarm blaring. Her room was dim, the only light coming from the soft morning glow peeking through her blinds. She groggily reached out and hit the snooze button, but the events of the previous evening were still fresh in her mind. There was a shift in the air, something she couldn't quite place yet, but it felt significant. Her mother's words had echoed in her thoughts long after they said goodbye last night. She was proud of her. Proud. It was a strange feeling— one that Leila had never really expected.

As she dragged herself out of bed and started getting ready for school, she found herself replaying the conversation in her head. Her mother was trying. She was trying, and maybe Leila was too. Maybe they could make it work. But a part of Leila still hesitated. Could she really trust that her mom had changed? Could things really be different this time?

Leila's phone buzzed on her desk. It was a message from Destiny, as usual.

"Good morning! Coffee?"

Leila smiled and quickly replied, "You read my mind."

Within minutes, she was grabbing her backpack and heading

out the door, ready for another day. As she walked down the quiet street toward the bus stop, her thoughts wandered again, this time to the coming school year. The event at the community center had left her feeling accomplished, but it also left a nagging feeling that there was more to figure out. The cracks in her relationship with her mom were deep, and though a small part of Leila hoped they could heal, she knew it wouldn't be easy.

At school, the day started like any other. Leila met Destiny by their lockers, her friend already sipping on a coffee. Destiny flashed a wide grin as she passed Leila her own cup.

"You good today?" Destiny asked, her tone light but concerned.

Leila took a sip of the hot, bitter coffee, feeling the warmth spread through her. "Yeah, I'm... I don't know. A little tired, but I'm good. Just thinking about things."

"Like your mom?" Destiny asked, raising an eyebrow.

Leila sighed and leaned against the lockers. "Yeah. I'm not sure what to think. I mean, she showed up yesterday. That's progress, right?"

"It's definitely something. But don't expect it to be all perfect just because she said she's trying." Destiny's voice was gentle but firm, as though she was speaking from experience.

"I know," Leila replied, "but... it's just different. She actually said she was proud of me. And for her to say that, after all this time, it's kind of huge."

Destiny gave her a reassuring smile. "I get that. But just make sure you don't hold your breath waiting for everything to be perfect. It's going to take time."

Leila nodded. She appreciated Destiny's honesty, even if it wasn't exactly what she wanted to hear. Sometimes, it felt like the world wanted her to move on, to leave the past behind, but it wasn't that easy.

The bell rang, signaling the start of the school day, and the friends fell into their usual rhythm, heading to their respective classes. Leila wasn't paying attention during her first-period lecture. She kept glancing at her phone, waiting for a message, anything, from her mom. She had left a text asking how her day was going, but the response hadn't come yet. Maybe she was just busy. Or maybe she just didn't know what to say.

Leila tried to push the thoughts out of her mind. It wasn't like she could do anything about it right now. She tried to focus on the lesson, the words drifting in and out of her consciousness, but her mind kept returning to the same place: the complex, fragile state of her relationship with her mom.

After school, Leila found herself walking home alone. Destiny had stayed after school for a club meeting, so Leila had the walk to herself. She let the sound of her sneakers tapping against the pavement settle her nerves, focusing on the rhythm of her steps as she made her way down the familiar street.

When she got home, the house was quiet. Her mom was in the kitchen, sorting through a pile of mail, her back turned to Leila. For a moment, Leila hesitated, unsure of how to approach the situation. Her mother hadn't texted her back, and the silence in the house felt heavy, charged with unspoken words.

"Mom?" Leila asked, stepping into the kitchen.

Her mother turned, offering a smile that seemed a little uncertain. "Hey, sweetie. How was school?"

Leila leaned against the counter, looking at her mother carefully. "It was fine. Just the usual stuff. How about you? How's work?"

"It's good," her mom replied, her eyes flicking briefly to the stack of bills on the table. "Busy, but good. I was thinking about what we talked about last night. And I just... I don't know how to fix everything, but I want to try."

Leila's heart skipped a beat. "You don't have to fix everything. I just want you to be here. That's enough for now."

Her mother's expression softened. "I know. And I will. I promise."

Leila didn't know if she believed her mother's words fully, but for the first time in a long time, she felt like maybe they could make progress. Maybe, just maybe, they could rebuild their relationship, even if it was one small step at a time.

As the day wore on, Leila found herself thinking less about her mother's promises and more about her own future. The uncertainty she had been carrying with her for so long didn't disappear overnight, but she felt like she was starting to carve out a path forward—one where she wasn't defined by her past. And as her mom made dinner in the kitchen, Leila realized that maybe healing didn't have to mean forgetting. Maybe it was about learning to live with what had happened and moving forward with hope.

She picked up her phone and sent a message to Destiny: *"Thanks for being there today. I needed you."*

A moment later, the reply came: *"Always. You're not alone, Leila."*

Leila smiled, a sense of comfort washing over her. As she sat down to dinner with her mom, she realized that things could change, even if it took time. And maybe that was enough.

The next few days passed in a blur. Leila's thoughts seemed constantly occupied with her mother's words, the weight of them lingering long after their conversations ended. It wasn't that Leila had expected an immediate change, but the mere acknowledgment that things could be different felt like a small victory. For so long, her life had been one of uncertainty and disappointment, where the truth of her mother's promises was often broken before they could even settle in. But this time was different. Her mother's sincerity was palpable, and Leila wasn't sure if she should trust it yet, but the glimmer of hope it sparked was undeniable.

As the weekend approached, Leila found herself spending more time at home than usual. She had always been the kind of person who preferred solitude, but lately, there was a sense of comfort in being around her mother. They still didn't talk about everything, and there were still awkward silences, but the tension had lessened. Leila no longer felt the need to constantly guard her emotions, expecting the worst. Instead, there was a quiet understanding between them.

Saturday afternoon found Leila sitting at the kitchen table, a half-drunk cup of coffee sitting in front of her as she flipped through an old notebook of hers. The pages were filled with random scribbles, half-formed thoughts, and dreams she hadn't dared to write down for years. Some of them were from when she was younger—when her aspirations still felt clear and reachable. The others were from the past year, written in the midst of the chaos that had consumed her world.

She stopped at one page, a sentence scrawled across the top that had caught her attention. *What happens when your foundation isn't solid?*

It was a question she had never really answered, but something in her wanted to understand now more than ever. Her foundation had always felt shaky, unstable, built on promises that were never kept, or expectations that no one could ever meet. Her relationship with her mom had always been like that: an unsteady balance between love and disappointment. But something had changed, and though it wasn't perfect, she could feel that shift deep within her.

The sound of footsteps behind her broke her concentration, and she turned to see her mom standing in the doorway.

"You're quiet today," her mom remarked softly.

Leila smiled faintly, pushing the notebook aside. "Just thinking."

Her mother stepped into the kitchen, leaning against the counter. "About what?"

Leila shrugged, looking down at her hands. "Just stuff. Life, I guess. I've been thinking a lot about... us."

Her mother's face softened. "I've been thinking about us too."

Leila glanced up, meeting her mother's eyes for a moment. It was the first time in a long time that there had been such openness between them. It felt fragile, like something that could easily break, but it was real.

"I don't know how to make up for everything I've done, Leila. I've let you down so many times, and I wish I could go back and do things differently," her mom said, her voice thick with emotion. "But I'm trying. I want to be better."

Leila's throat tightened, and she found it hard to speak. Her mother had always been quick to apologize, but there was something different about the sincerity in her voice this time. It wasn't just words; it was an effort. Her mother was finally putting in the work to be a better parent, and for the first time, Leila could feel it.

"I know," Leila said quietly, surprised at how calm she felt despite the emotional storm brewing inside her. "I know you're trying. I'm... I'm trying too."

There was a moment of silence between them, and it felt as if everything that had been left unsaid over the years had finally found a way to come to the surface. The hurt and confusion, the love and the resentment, all swirling together in a messy, beautiful truth that neither of them had the words for. But for the first time in a long time, Leila didn't feel the need to hide behind her anger. She didn't have all the answers, but maybe they could figure this out together.

"I'm glad you're here, Mom," Leila whispered, feeling the weight in her chest lighten ever so slightly.

Her mom's eyes glistened as she walked over to Leila, pulling her into an unexpected embrace. "I'm glad you're here too."

Later that evening, after dinner, Leila found herself outside on the porch, her phone in hand. She sent a quick message to Destiny, who had been her rock through all the uncertainty.

"Hey, can we talk?"

Moments later, the reply came: *"Of course. What's up?"*

Leila took a deep breath, thinking carefully about what she wanted to say.

"I think things with my mom are starting to get better. We had a real conversation today. It feels different, but I'm scared it's too good to be true."

She didn't have to wait long for Destiny's response. *"I'm proud of you, Leila. Just take it one day at a time. You deserve peace. And if anyone can make it through this, it's you."*

Leila smiled at the message, feeling the weight of her fears ease slightly. She wasn't sure where this journey would lead, but for the first time, she felt like she was on the right path. It was a journey that would take time, and there would undoubtedly be bumps along the way, but she was beginning to understand something crucial: that healing wasn't about erasing the past. It was about facing it and choosing to move forward.

As the days went on, Leila found herself thinking less about the hurt her mother had caused and more about the future they could build. It wasn't going to be easy, and there would be moments of doubt, but it was a chance. A chance for both of them to redefine what family could mean. And for Leila, that was enough—for now.

By the end of the week, her mom surprised her with a small gesture—a scrapbook she had put together filled with old photos and memories. It was a simple thing, but it was a sign. Her mom was trying, really trying, to make up for the time they had lost. Leila didn't know what the future held, but for the first time in years, she felt something she hadn't felt in a long time: hope.

Chapter 6
Crossing the Line

Leila had always believed that certain things in life were meant to remain separate: school, home, friends, and family. Keeping these parts of her life compartmentalized had been a way for her to maintain control, to manage the overwhelming complexity of her world. But recently, it had felt like those boundaries were starting to blur. There were moments when she could no longer escape the intersection of all the things she had once kept so neatly separated, and the pressure of it was suffocating.

One such moment came on a Tuesday afternoon in the school parking lot. Leila had just finished her final class of the day and was walking toward her car when she saw Destiny leaning against the side of her truck, phone in hand. Her best friend had been absent for the past few days, caught up in something she wasn't talking about, and the absence had only added to Leila's growing unease.

"Hey," Leila called out, walking over with a hesitant smile.

Destiny looked up, her expression unreadable. "Hey," she

replied, her voice flat.

"What's going on? You've been MIA," Leila asked, a slight frown tugging at her brow. She had noticed that Destiny's demeanor had shifted in the last few days, becoming quieter, more distant. The usual spark in her eyes was gone, replaced by a cool, guarded look that didn't sit right with Leila.

Destiny shifted her weight, eyes glancing away for a moment before locking with Leila's. "Just... stuff," she muttered, not offering any further explanation.

Leila didn't buy it. Destiny was her closest friend, the person who had always been there for her, but this? This felt different. There was something weighing on her that she wasn't willing to share, and that made Leila anxious.

"Come on, Destiny. We've always been able to talk about things. If something's going on, you can tell me," Leila said, her voice softer now, trying to reassure her friend. Destiny was always the one who helped her navigate her feelings, the one who made her feel like she wasn't alone in the world. And yet, now it seemed like the roles had reversed.

"I know, I know," Destiny replied, her gaze dropping to the ground. "But I don't want to drag you into it."

Leila stepped closer, her brow furrowing. "Drag me into what? What's going on?"

Destiny shook her head, finally looking up at Leila with a sadness in her eyes that was hard to ignore. "It's complicated. And I don't know how to explain it."

Leila's heart began to race. There was a part of her that feared the worst—that Destiny was in trouble or struggling in ways Leila couldn't comprehend. But she refused to let that fear control her. "You don't have to explain everything, but I'm here for you, no matter what."

Destiny seemed to hesitate, her fingers playing with the edge of her jacket sleeve. Finally, after what felt like an eternity, she sighed and spoke again, her voice tinged with guilt. "I've been dealing with some stuff with my family. My dad... he's been going through a rough patch, and it's been hard to watch. I don't know what's going to happen, and I've just been trying to process it all."

Leila's heart softened, and she moved closer, placing a hand on Destiny's shoulder. "I'm sorry. I didn't know." The realization that her friend had been quietly bearing such a heavy burden made Leila feel guilty for not having noticed sooner. They'd always shared everything, but in the chaos of her own life—her mother's slow attempts at healing, the pressure at school—she hadn't stopped to really check in with Destiny.

Destiny smiled faintly, but there was no real warmth in it. "It's not your fault. It's just... hard. I don't know what to do anymore. I feel like I'm losing control of everything."

Leila's heart ached for her friend. Destiny had always been the strong one, the one who could laugh in the face of adversity. But now, she seemed fragile, broken in a way Leila couldn't fully understand.

"You don't have to have everything figured out," Leila said softly. "I'm here for you. We'll get through this together."

For a moment, there was silence between them, a quiet understanding passing in the air. Destiny's eyes softened as she let out a breath she hadn't known she'd been holding. "Thanks, Leila. I don't know what I'd do without you."

Leila smiled, but inside, she felt a growing sense of unease. Destiny was opening up, yes—but there was still so much left unsaid. And as much as she wanted to help, there was a part of her that wasn't sure if she could. She didn't know how to help her friend navigate this new territory of pain and uncertainty, just as she wasn't sure how to handle the changes in her own life.

But as they walked to their cars, Leila couldn't shake the feeling that everything was about to change. They were no longer the same people they had been a year ago. Destiny's struggles were real, Leila's own journey with her mother was still unfolding, and the balance between everything—school, friends, family—was growing more complicated with each passing day.

Leila had always thought that the hardest part of growing up was dealing with the academic pressures, and the expectations of others. But now, she understood that the true difficulty lay in learning how to navigate the complexities of relationships—the ones you thought were solid, the ones that seemed like they could weather any storm. And when those relationships began to crack, when the lines between them blurred, you were left to question everything.

"Hey," Destiny said, breaking Leila's thoughts as she climbed into her car. "Maybe we can hang out this weekend? I could use some distraction."

Leila smiled, relief flooding her chest. "I'd like that. We'll figure it out, okay?"

"Okay," Destiny replied, and for the first time in days, her voice held a note of hope.

As Leila drove home later that afternoon, she couldn't help but think about the shifting nature of her friendships, the fragility of trust, and how the people she loved most were changing right before her eyes. It was like watching a house settle—slowly, imperceptibly, until one day you noticed the cracks in the foundation.

And she wasn't sure if she was ready to face what came next.

As the week went on, Leila couldn't shake the unease that had settled in her chest. The conversation with Destiny lingered in her mind, like a puzzle with missing pieces. Destiny had always been the one to have it all together—funny, outgoing, and confident. But now, there was something hidden beneath the surface, something she hadn't fully revealed. Leila knew that the tough exterior Destiny showed to the world was only part of the story. But she also understood that, sometimes, people weren't ready to let others in, even when they were falling apart on the inside.

Friday evening arrived before Leila had a chance to fully process everything. She had spent the week distracted—spending time with her mom, attempting to study for an upcoming test, and checking in with Destiny, but always sensing that something was off. It was only when she received a text from Destiny that her heart began to settle a bit.

Hey, are you still up for hanging out tomorrow?

Leila felt a rush of relief. She knew Destiny hadn't been in the best headspace lately, but it was a small victory that her friend was still reaching out, still wanting to spend time together.

Absolutely. Let's do something fun. Maybe a movie night?

Destiny's response was quick.

Sounds perfect. You pick the movie.

Leila smiled. It felt good to have something simple to look forward to. For a while now, the only thing that seemed to ground her was time spent with Destiny, even if the conversation wasn't always easy.

Saturday came, and Leila arrived at Destiny's house just as the sun began to dip below the horizon. The cool evening air carried a promise of fall—crisp and refreshing, with the scent of leaves and distant bonfires in the air. She pulled into the driveway, seeing Destiny's familiar truck parked near the front door.

Stepping out of her car, Leila grabbed her purse and walked up to the front door. She knocked lightly before pushing it open, not waiting for an invitation. Destiny's house was always open to her.

Inside, Destiny was already sitting on the couch, wearing her usual oversized hoodie and a pair of sweatpants. Her hair was pulled back in a messy bun, and she was scrolling through her phone. She didn't look up when Leila entered.

"Hey," Leila said with a grin. "Movie night, right?"

Destiny gave a small smile, putting her phone down. "Yeah, I figured it was time to finally do something normal."

"Normal's good," Leila replied, settling onto the couch beside her. "We need a break from all the heavy stuff, right?"

"Yeah," Destiny said, her voice quieter this time. She didn't meet Leila's gaze, her focus seemingly drawn to the screen ahead. Leila felt the weight of the unspoken words between them. Destiny had been trying to pretend everything was okay, but Leila knew better. There were too many cracks, too much she was still keeping to herself.

"You don't have to pretend with me," Leila said, her voice soft but firm.

Destiny sighed, finally turning to face her. Her eyes were tired, a dullness to them that hadn't been there before. "I don't know what's going on with me, Leila. It's like I'm living in this fog, and I can't find a way out."

Leila's heart hurt for her friend. She hated seeing Destiny like this—so vulnerable, so lost. The girl who was always so full of energy, always the first to crack a joke or take charge in any situation, now seemed like a shadow of herself.

"You don't have to have all the answers," Leila said quietly. "But you don't have to do this alone."

Destiny bit her lip, looking away for a moment. "I don't want to drag you into it, Leila. I don't want you to worry about me."

Leila shook her head. "It's too late for that. You're my best friend. I'm here, no matter what."

Destiny swallowed hard as if trying to hold back emotions she wasn't ready to face. "I know you are. It's just... I'm scared, Leila. I don't know what's going to happen. And I don't want to disappoint anyone."

The honesty in Destiny's voice made Leila's heartache. She couldn't imagine what it would feel like to carry the weight of that kind of fear, to feel like you were constantly on the edge of letting everyone down. But she understood now that the girl sitting beside her was holding on to more than just her family's troubles. There were layers, deeper struggles that Destiny wasn't ready to share yet.

"You don't have to be perfect," Leila said, her voice steady. "You're allowed to be scared. You're allowed to be a little lost sometimes. And you don't have to have it all figured out. I don't, either."

Destiny turned to face her, her eyes glassy. She opened her mouth, as if to say something, but closed it again, her lips trembling.

Leila reached out, placing a hand on her friend's arm. "You're not alone in this, okay? You don't have to hide it from me. Whatever you need, I'm here."

For a long moment, Destiny just stared at her, as if processing everything that had been said. Then, finally, she nodded. It wasn't a complete solution. It wasn't the end of the road or a magic fix, but it was a small step in the right direction.

"Thanks, Leila," she whispered.

Leila squeezed her friend's arm. "Anytime."

They sat in silence for a moment, the air between them comfortable, yet heavy with everything that hadn't been said. The movie, forgotten, played quietly in the background, but neither of them seemed to care. Sometimes, just being there for each other was enough.

Eventually, Destiny let out a small sigh and smiled, though it was a little weary. "Okay, I'm done being a downer. Movie time?"

Leila grinned. "Absolutely. But I get to pick this time."

Destiny rolled her eyes, but the corners of her mouth tugged up in the slightest of smiles. "Fine. But it better not be a rom-com."

Leila laughed. "No promises."

As they settled into the couch together, the tension between them eased. It was a slow process—this rebuilding, this healing—but Leila knew they were moving in the right direction. Whatever lay ahead, they would face it together.

As the evening wore on, the movie faded into the background, its sounds drowned out by the quiet conversations between Leila and Destiny. They didn't talk about the heavy things again—not yet. But there was an unspoken understanding that the walls between them were starting to crack. Destiny's earlier smile, even if small and fleeting, was a sign that she wasn't as lost as she had appeared to be earlier in the week. She wasn't fixed, and neither was Leila, but tonight was about small steps, not grand gestures.

Leila glanced over at her friend, who had finally relaxed, her arms stretched out on the back of the couch, her legs tucked up beneath her. The tension in Destiny's posture had eased, and she had even laughed a few times at the jokes in the movie, a sound that had been missing for too long. It was moments like these that reminded Leila of how much she valued this friendship, even if it sometimes felt like they were walking through mud, inch by inch, toward something better.

"Okay, so, what's the real deal?" Leila asked, her voice teasing but filled with warmth. Destiny raised an eyebrow but didn't respond immediately. Leila could see the hesitation in her friend's eyes, but Destiny didn't shy away. She was trying to figure out how to let someone in.

"About what?" Destiny finally asked, a slight smirk on her face, though Leila could tell it wasn't a genuine one.

Leila shrugged, not backing down. "About everything. The stuff that's been going on with you. I know there's more you're not telling me. But I get it if you're not ready to talk about it yet." She paused, letting the words hang in the air. "Just know I'm here when you are."

Destiny remained silent for a long time, staring at the TV but not really watching. She had gotten quiet again, and Leila wondered if she had pushed too hard, too fast. Maybe she needed more time. But as the minutes ticked by, Leila could feel the silence growing heavier. Destiny was wrestling with something—something bigger than the weight of high school, friendships, or even the pressure of trying to meet expectations.

"I don't know if I can explain it, Leila," Destiny said finally, her voice small. It wasn't what Leila had expected, and for a moment, she wasn't sure how to respond. Destiny had always been the one with the words—able to speak her mind without hesitation. But now, her vulnerability felt raw, like she was reaching out for something, unsure if it would be there to catch her.

Leila shifted, sitting up a little straighter on the couch. "You don't have to explain it all, but you don't have to keep it inside either," she said gently. "You can tell me when you're ready."

Destiny let out a shaky breath, her fingers fiddling with the hem of her hoodie. "I don't even know where to start. It's not just one thing, Leila. It's everything. It's feeling like I'm not good enough, like I'm constantly disappointing everyone. Like I don't belong anywhere... like I'm just a mess, and I don't know how to fix it."

Leila's heart ached for her friend. She could see it now—the fear of being exposed, the fear of not measuring up to the people in Destiny's life. Leila had never seen it before, but it was there, clear as day.

"You're not a mess," Leila said firmly, reaching over to gently place a hand on Destiny's arm. "You're allowed to feel all of that. I don't care about the things you think are 'wrong' with you. I care about you."

Destiny's eyes flickered with emotion as she looked at Leila, her defenses crumbling little by little. "I don't know if I believe that. I don't know if I believe I'm enough."

"You are," Leila insisted. "And if you ever doubt that again, I'll remind you. We're friends, remember? It's what we do."

Destiny's lips quivered as she gave a shaky laugh. "I've always been the one who's supposed to have it all together. I don't even know how to let anyone in anymore."

Leila squeezed her arm, giving her a reassuring smile. "It's okay to let go sometimes. It's okay to ask for help. You don't have to carry everything by yourself."

The words hung in the air for a while, and for the first time that evening, Destiny didn't immediately deflect. She didn't try to hide behind humor or her usual confident bravado. Instead, she seemed to sink deeper into the moment, her eyes searching Leila's face, looking for something—comfort, perhaps, or validation. Destiny was always the one giving, always the one offering support. But at this moment, she needed it, and Leila was determined to give it to her.

"Do you think... do you think that you could ever forgive me?" Destiny asked quietly, her voice shaky.

Leila's eyebrows furrowed. "Forgive you? What for?"

Destiny swallowed hard. "For all the times I've let you down. For the times I've been too wrapped up in my own stuff to be a real friend. I've been... distant. And I hate that about myself."

Leila's heart swelled at the rawness of Destiny's words. "You don't have to apologize for being human, Destiny. We've all been there. I get it. I've been there, too. And I don't need perfection from you. I just need you to be you."

Destiny blinked rapidly, a tear finally slipping down her cheek. She quickly wiped it away, but Leila saw it—saw how much the weight of everything had been building up. This wasn't just about the surface-level stress of high school or everyday struggles. This was about self-doubt, about feeling like she wasn't enough, about battling inner demons that no one else could see.

Leila moved closer, wrapping her arm around Destiny's shoulders. "I'm not going anywhere. You don't have to do this alone."

For a moment, Destiny didn't say anything. But then, her shoulders shook with quiet sobs, and Leila held her tighter. The movie still played in the background, but all of it seemed insignificant compared to the quiet release that Destiny was finally allowing herself. She had been carrying so much, trying to appear strong when she was anything but.

"You're going to be okay," Leila whispered, her voice calm and steady. "You're going to get through this. We're going to get through this."

Destiny's breathing evened out as she rested her head on Leila's shoulder, and for the first time in a long time, Leila felt like things were starting to fall into place. It wouldn't happen overnight, and it wouldn't be easy. But this—this moment of vulnerability and connection—was the beginning of something stronger than the silence that had separated them before.

And Leila would be there every step of the way.

The room fell into a comfortable silence, save for the soft hum of the movie still playing on the screen. Destiny's breathing had steadied, and the tension that had filled the space earlier had loosened. It wasn't fixed; things weren't suddenly perfect, but in that moment, it felt like a turning point.

Leila sat still, careful not to disturb the fragile peace they had found. She felt a sense of relief wash over her, as though a weight had been lifted. Destiny, her best friend, was finally letting herself be vulnerable, and Leila was there to catch her. This was what they had needed—a real conversation, without distractions, without the facades they'd both been hiding behind.

The minutes ticked by, and Destiny's head remained nestled against Leila's shoulder. It was an unspoken promise, a silent agreement that no matter what, they would face whatever came next together. Leila wasn't sure what the future held, but for the first time in a long time, she felt certain that they would be okay.

"I'm sorry for being so distant," Destiny said again, her voice barely above a whisper. She hadn't fully pulled away, but she had shifted slightly, her face now turned toward Leila.

"You don't have to apologize," Leila replied softly, her fingers tracing small circles on Destiny's arm. "You've been going through a lot. You don't owe me anything."

Destiny gave a small, bittersweet smile. "It's just... sometimes it feels like everything I do, I mess it up. I push people away without even realizing it."

Leila squeezed her shoulder gently. "You don't mess up, Destiny. You've just been carrying too much on your own. You're allowed to have bad days, to feel like you're not okay. That doesn't mean you're a failure. It just means you're human."

Destiny exhaled slowly, her breath shaky as if she was still trying to come to terms with the emotions swirling inside her. "I never realized how much I needed someone to say that."

Leila looked at her with a gentle, reassuring smile. "That's what friends are for, right?"

Destiny nodded, her eyes still a little glassy, but there was a flicker of something softer in them now—a recognition that maybe, just maybe, she didn't have to do everything alone.

The movie continued in the background, but neither of them paid attention to it anymore. It had become background noise to the real conversation they were having—the one that mattered most.

A few minutes passed before Destiny pulled away slightly, her eyes scanning the room as if she was finding her bearings again. She still looked tired, but there was clarity in her eyes now, as though she had just let out a breath she had been holding for far too long.

"I didn't know where to start, but now it feels... easier," Destiny said quietly, her gaze shifting back to Leila.

Leila nodded. "Yeah, it's not about having all the answers. It's just about being here for each other. And when you're ready to talk more, I'll be ready to listen."

"I'm not sure I'm ready to talk about everything yet," Destiny admitted, her voice soft. "But I'll get there. I just need time."

Leila gave a supportive smile. "That's okay. We'll take it one step at a time."

Destiny's expression softened, and she reached for Leila's hand, a gesture that spoke volumes. "Thank you for sticking around. For not giving up on me. I don't deserve it."

Leila shook her head quickly. "You don't need to earn my friendship. I'm not going anywhere."

For a moment, it felt as if everything had shifted. The tension between them, the unspoken distance, was slowly starting to fade. They were on the same page now, not perfect but moving in the right direction. Destiny still had a long way to go, and Leila knew that. But tonight was a small victory.

"So," Leila said, trying to lighten the mood a little. "What do you think about watching the rest of the movie, or is it officially ruined?"

Destiny chuckled softly, wiping at her eyes. "I think we can salvage it. But no promises about paying attention."

Leila grinned, grateful for the humor that had returned. "I'll take it."

They settled back into the couch, a comfortable quiet settling over them again, but this time, it felt different. There was no awkwardness, no tension. Just two friends, sitting in the warmth of their shared understanding.

As the movie played on, they occasionally glanced at each other, exchanging knowing smiles or laughing at the occasional funny scene. But the real story was unfolding between them, in the way they communicated without words, in the way they had begun to heal from the silence that had once threatened to pull them apart.

And when the movie ended, the clock on the wall told them it was late. Destiny stretched out, yawning as she pushed herself up from the couch.

"I should probably get going," Destiny said, her voice quieter now, more at peace. "I've got a ton of homework to do."

Leila stood up as well, but she didn't want to let this moment end. "Hey, take care of yourself, okay? If you need anything, you know where to find me."

Destiny smiled, the warmth in her eyes unmistakable. "Thanks, Leila. Really."

They stood there for a moment, just looking at each other before Destiny gave her a quick hug. It wasn't long, but it was enough. Leila held on just a little longer, wishing she could take away all the pain and fear Destiny had been carrying, but knowing she couldn't do that. All she could do was be there, and for now, that was enough.

As Destiny walked out the door, Leila couldn't help but feel a sense of hope. There was no magic cure for everything that had happened, but tonight, things had shifted. They were moving toward something better, and Leila was determined to be by Destiny's side every step of the way.

Leila closed the door softly behind her and leaned back against it, taking a deep breath. For the first time in a long while, she felt like things were going to be okay.

And that, in itself, was a victory.

As the evening continued, the weight that had burdened Destiny seemed to lift bit by bit, like fog dissipating with the first rays of the sun. The apartment was quiet, save for the occasional sound of the wind against the windows, but Leila didn't mind. The silence wasn't uncomfortable anymore. It felt peaceful, a space where both of them could just breathe without the pressure to perform or pretend.

Leila moved to the kitchen, gathering the last of the dishes. Destiny hadn't left yet, but there was no rush. There was a comfort in knowing they didn't have to fill every moment with conversation. It was enough to just exist together. The occasional glance between them spoke volumes, a silent agreement that, no matter the uncertainties ahead, they were in this together.

After a few minutes, Destiny returned to the couch, her backpack slung over her shoulder. She paused for a moment before speaking again, her voice a little more sure than before.

"I never told you this," Destiny said, her eyes on the ground, "but sometimes, I feel like I don't belong anywhere. Like no matter how hard I try, I'm always one step behind, never quite getting it right."

Leila paused, setting the last plate down and turning toward her friend. "What do you mean?" she asked softly, stepping closer.

Destiny looked up, a small smile tugging at the corner of her lips. "I don't know. I just... feel like I'm always on the outside looking in, you know? Like everyone has it together but me."

Leila walked over, sitting beside her on the couch. She could see the uncertainty in Destiny's eyes, the vulnerability that had taken so long to emerge. "I get that," Leila said quietly. "I've felt that way too, sometimes. No matter how hard I try, I'm just... not enough. But you know what? I think everyone feels that way, at least a little. It's not a sign that you're failing. It's just a part of growing up."

Destiny gave a small nod, looking comforted by Leila's words. It wasn't a magical fix, but it was something. For the first time in a long time, she felt like she didn't have to face it alone.

They sat in comfortable silence for a while longer before Destiny spoke again, her voice quieter now. "I never meant to push you away, you know? It's just... sometimes, I get so wrapped up in everything that I forget to reach out. I forget that I have people who care about me."

Leila reached over, taking Destiny's hand in her own. "I know. And I understand. But you don't have to do this alone. You don't have to carry all of it on your own shoulders. You're not a burden, Destiny. You never were."

For the first time in a while, Destiny let herself believe those words. She squeezed Leila's hand, a silent promise that she wouldn't let herself push away the people who cared about her. It was going to take time, but she was ready to start. And maybe, just maybe, she could begin to feel like she belonged.

Destiny stood up, stretching her arms over her head. "I should get going. I've got homework to catch up on, and I don't want to stay up too late."

Leila nodded, following her friend to the door. "Okay, but remember what I said. You're never alone in this. You can always talk to me, no matter what."

Destiny smiled a soft but genuine smile and gave Leila a hug before heading out the door. "Thanks for everything, Leila. I really mean it."

Leila watched her friend walk down the hallway, the weight in her chest feeling lighter than it had all evening. Things weren't perfect—far from it—but they were moving forward. And that was enough for now.

As she closed the door behind her, Leila let out a breath she hadn't realized she'd been holding. The evening had been exhausting, and emotionally draining, but it had also been one of the most important moments in their relationship. They were healing, slowly but surely.

Leila moved back to the couch and sank into the cushions, feeling a sense of relief flood through her. It wasn't just Destiny who had learned something that evening. For the longest time, she had been afraid of pushing too hard, afraid that if she kept reaching out, she would only push Destiny further away. But she realized that sometimes, it was about showing up and being present, even when things were messy. Leila had come to terms with her own feelings, too.

Chapter 7
Distance is a Quiet Thing

Leila first noticed it in the tiniest shifts—so small she might've missed them if she hadn't known Destiny so well. The way their texts got shorter. The way the "lmao"s turned to "lol"s, then to nothing at all. The way Destiny started replying with a single word when before she'd send paragraphs, rants, midnight voice notes full of laughter or whispered secrets. At first, Leila chalked it up to stress. Senior year was chaotic for everyone. College decisions were rolling in, graduation requirements loomed like storm clouds, and Destiny's home life had never been simple. She told herself Destiny just needed space.

But then came the dodged hangouts. The *"Sorry, something came up"* text when they were supposed to go for coffee. The "forgot to respond" moments that didn't quite feel accidental. The way Destiny stopped waiting at her locker. The way she started disappearing in the crowd before Leila could even say hi.

And just like that, what used to feel easy started feeling like a guessing game. Like walking on the edge of something that might break.

Leila sat in the cafeteria on Monday, her lunch tray untouched in front of her. The pasta was congealed and lukewarm, curling at the edges like it knew it was unwanted. She pushed it around with her fork, not really seeing it. Her eyes kept drifting toward the cafeteria entrance, catching every movement, every backpack, every girl with curly hair who wasn't Destiny.

Destiny wasn't coming. Leila knew that.

Still, she looked.

It was pathetic, probably. She hated that she cared this much. Hated the knot in her stomach that had been tightening with every day Destiny pulled further away. And what made it worse—so much worse—was that Leila didn't even know why. She replayed everything in her mind over and over again like a glitchy movie reel.

That night at Destiny's house.

The rain had been soft against the windows, a background hum as they watched some cheesy rom-com they didn't even pretend to care about. Destiny had been quiet—quieter than usual—but Leila hadn't pushed. She'd just sat beside her, their legs pressed together, shoulders touching. When Destiny finally broke down, when the words about her dad came spilling out, jagged and raw, Leila had done the only thing that felt right—she held her.

They stayed like that for hours, the movie forgotten. Leila had threaded her fingers with Destiny's, and Destiny hadn't pulled away. If anything, she held tighter. Her head had rested on Leila's shoulder, breaths soft, eyes glassy but peaceful. Leila remembered thinking—*This means something. It has to.* And maybe she'd imagined it, but there was a moment when Destiny looked at her—really looked—and something passed between them. Not friendship. Not exactly.

Something else.

But now, Destiny was avoiding her like that moment never happened.

Leila's thumb hovered over her phone screen, staring at the last message she'd typed but hadn't sent. She'd written it four different ways already. Too casual, too dramatic, too desperate. Finally, she settled on something honest.

Hey. I miss you. Want to hang out this weekend? Just us?

She hit send before she could talk herself out of it.

The moment it was gone, a pit opened in her stomach.

She locked her phone and shoved it into her backpack, forcing herself to sit up straighter. She wouldn't cry in the cafeteria. She wouldn't give this feeling more power than it already had.

"Mind if I sit?" came a voice, light and a little amused.

Leila looked up to see Micah standing across from her, tray in hand, his ever-present copy of *Beloved* tucked under his arm like it was part of him. He was grinning, eyes curious but not pushy.

"Go for it," she said, waving to the empty seat.

Micah dropped into the chair and set his tray down. He looked at her with an expression that was equal parts amusement and mild concern. "You know, I think your lunch might be trying to stage a rebellion."

Leila blinked, then followed his gaze to her pasta. She let out a weak laugh. "It's lost the will to live."

"Well, good thing I brought backup," he said, sliding his tray slightly toward her. "Fry?"

She took one without arguing and popped it into her mouth. "Thanks."

They settled into small talk. Micah was easy to talk to—he always had been. They'd been in AP Lit together since last year, but it was only this semester that he started seeking her out. He had a laid-back vibe, the kind of person who made you feel interesting just by listening. He asked her about her take on the final essay, and when she made a joke about hating Plath and loving her at the same time, he laughed like she'd said the most brilliant thing in the world.

She smiled. She laughed. She felt her body relaxing for the first time in days.

But it was a lie.

Because even as she laughed with Micah, her eyes flicked to the cafeteria entrance.

Even as she smiled, part of her was screaming: *Why won't you just text me back?*

And then—like the universe had heard her—Destiny appeared.

She was walking in with a group Leila didn't recognize, her hoodie sleeves pushed up, phone in her hand. She wasn't laughing, but she was talking, animated in a way that made Leila's stomach tighten. She hadn't seen that version of Destiny in days. Not since their night on the couch. Not since the silence began.

Destiny's eyes scanned the room as she walked. And then they landed on Leila.

Leila didn't look away.

Neither did Destiny.

It was a heartbeat. Maybe two.

A moment heavy with all the words they hadn't said.

Then Destiny's gaze dropped. She looked away.

And that—somehow—hurt more than if she'd never looked at all.

Leila looked down at her tray after Destiny looked away, the half-smile she'd been holding collapsing as quickly as it had risen. Her heart beat too loudly in her ears. She told herself not to read into it—that maybe Destiny had just been surprised to see her, or maybe she'd just been looking past her. But the heat in her chest said otherwise. It said that Destiny saw her and chose not to stay in that moment.

Micah, oblivious to the silent battle that had just played out across the room, tossed another fry into his mouth and started talking about their Lit essay. Something about how the concept of duality in The Bell Jar reminded him of what it felt like to be stuck in between versions of yourself. Leila nodded and even managed a chuckle at one of his analogies, but it was all auto-pilot.

She felt split—half of her sitting at this table, laughing with someone kind and attentive, and the other half still standing in Destiny's hallway, replaying the warmth of fingers intertwined on a couch two weeks ago.

That night haunted her like a ghost. And she didn't know how to explain it to anyone else—how something as simple as a shared silence could mean everything. How it wasn't about a kiss or even about saying the words, but about what was there in the spaces between.

Micah waved a hand in front of her face. "Earth to Leila. You with me?"

She blinked, realizing she had spaced out completely. "Sorry. Yeah. Just tired."

Micah nodded slowly, his expression softening. "You want to study later this week? I figured we could knock out that essay outline together."

Leila hesitated. Not because she didn't want to hang out with him. But because it felt like saying yes was choosing something—choosing not to wait. Not to hope. And that scared her more than she wanted to admit.

"Sure," she said finally. "Thursday?"

"Thursday works," he said with a grin.

They cleaned up their trays together, and Micah walked with her toward class. She appreciated the way he didn't try too hard—he wasn't putting pressure on her to perform or to be anything other than what she was: emotionally wrecked and pretending not to be. When they got to the doors of AP Lit, he held one open for her like a cliché, but it made her smile.

"You're full of surprises," she said, brushing past him.

Micah chuckled. "Only the charming kind, I hope."

Leila didn't respond. She just slid into her seat and pulled out her notebook, not quite ready to feel what she was feeling.

The next day passed in a blur. Classes. Hallway noise. Teachers reminding everyone about deadlines and cap-and-gown pickups. Leila went through the motions. She answered questions when called on. She took notes she didn't process. She made it to lunch and back without seeing Destiny once, which was somehow both a relief and a disappointment.

She got home late that evening after helping her mom with errands, and when she dropped her backpack on her bedroom floor, she collapsed onto her bed with a sigh. Her body ached with a tiredness that wasn't physical. It was emotional. Existential. The ache of caring too much about something—or someone—who wasn't giving you anything back.

She opened her phone, hesitated, then went to Destiny's thread. Her last message—"Want to hang out this weekend?"—still sat there. Unread.

Still.

Her thumb hovered over the keyboard. For a moment, she thought about deleting the thread altogether. Erasing it like erasing the texts would erase the feelings. But instead, she swiped back and opened her photo gallery.

There they were.

Screenshots of late-night memes. Pictures of Destiny from their hike last fall—Destiny standing on a rock with her arms spread wide, Leila's jacket wrapped around her shoulders. A blurry selfie of them both laughing so hard neither could keep their eyes open. A video of Destiny singing off-key in the car.

Leila watched it twice. Then a third time.

She missed her.

But what kind of person vanishes after that kind of night?

What kind of person holds your hand and cries into your shoulder and then just... leaves?

Her phone buzzed, and she jolted, heart leaping.

Micah.

Hey, Thursday still good? I'll bring snacks.

Her heart dropped a little. Not because she didn't want to study with Micah. But because she was still waiting for a different name to light up her screen.

She stared at the text for a while before responding.

Yeah. That works. Thanks.

She hit send. Then threw her phone across the bed and pulled a pillow over her face.

God, what was wrong with her?

Thursday arrived faster than she expected. The weather was warm in that strange in-between way where it felt like spring but still hinted at cold around the edges. She and Micah met up in the library like they'd planned, and for once, she tried to let herself be present.

He brought Twizzlers and sour gummies, which made her

laugh. They joked about the weird metaphors in Plath's poetry, debated over their favorite book-to-movie adaptations, and teased each other over font preferences for their essay outline.

And for a little while, she actually felt okay.

But then, as they were packing up, Leila looked toward the window—and froze.

Destiny.

Walking past the quad, alone, headphones in.

She wasn't looking their way. She was just passing by, her hair half-up, her hoodie sleeves pushed to her elbows. There was something different about her posture. Guarded. Like she was holding everything inside.

Micah noticed her change in expression. "You okay?"

Leila nodded quickly, pretending to focus on her binder. "Yeah. Just spaced out."

She glanced back. Destiny was already gone.

It was like seeing a ghost. One that didn't know she'd died.

And Leila didn't know if she should mourn her or go chasing after what was left.

The halls of Eastridge High were loud with spring. Promposals were happening every day—some grand, some awkward, some involving balloons or ukuleles or poster boards with bad puns. Graduation announcements were being mailed out. Class rings were arriving in tiny velvet boxes. College acceptance letters and scholarship offers danced through conversations like confetti.

But for Leila, everything felt gray.

It wasn't just Destiny. It was the way everything was moving forward around her, while she remained frozen in place. There were people laughing in every hallway, people planning senior pranks and arguing about cap-decorating rules, and yet all of it blurred into the background like white noise. Leila was present, but detached. She showed up to class. She turned in her assignments. She even managed a few laughs when Micah was around.

But inside? She felt like a house mid-collapse. The kind that looked fine from a distance but was quietly splitting apart beneath the drywall.

She didn't see Destiny that much anymore. Not really. She caught flashes—her back turned at her locker, her laugh down the hall, her presence like perfume you only noticed after it was gone. Sometimes their eyes met. Once or twice, Destiny even gave a tiny wave. But it was always from a distance. Never enough to mean anything.

And that hurt more than silence.

It said: I know you're there. I'm choosing not to come closer.

Leila didn't wave back.

She stopped looking altogether.

She walked past Destiny one morning, their shoulders almost brushing, and didn't turn her head. It felt like rebellion. Like reclaiming some sliver of power she'd given away.

In AP Lit, Micah slid into the seat beside her again. He didn't ask anymore. It had become unspoken, and oddly, that was a comfort. He never demanded answers from her. Never poked at the places that hurt.

That afternoon, as Mr. Keenan rambled about postmodernism and the "madwoman archetype," Micah slipped her a note. Old school, folded twice over, passed across the desk like something from a 90s teen movie.

Leila opened it under the table. His handwriting was careful, all uppercase:

You seem kinda sad. If you ever need to talk (or vent or rage scream), I'm good at listening.

Leila stared at it for a few seconds, then folded it up and slid it into her notebook without responding. She didn't know what to say. Not because she didn't appreciate the kindness, but because she didn't trust herself not to break if she let someone else hold her pieces.

After class, Micah didn't bring it up. He just smiled and walked beside her down the hall, talking about some band he'd found on a subreddit she'd never heard of. She smiled at the right parts, nodded at the right times. But her mind was somewhere else.

It always was.

That night, Leila sat in her bedroom with her laptop open but untouched, her half-written paper blinking on a blank document. Instead of working, she found herself scrolling through Instagram, her thumb moving mechanically across the screen.

And then she saw it.

Destiny's story.

A backyard party. String lights. Paper lanterns. Someone had a guitar, and a group of girls were laughing at a joke the camera hadn't caught. But it was the last post that froze her.

It was Destiny and Jayla—shoulder to shoulder, cheeks pressed close, both grinning like they didn't have a care in the world. Jayla's hand was around Destiny's waist.

The caption read:

Vibes only. Pink heart. Music note. Champagne emoji.

Leila didn't feel jealous. That would've made it easier. Cleaner.

What she felt was worse.

She felt disposable.

Like someone who had been essential for a moment but was now an afterthought.

She clicked the mute button on Destiny's profile without hesitation. No drama. No announcement. Just silence.

She closed the app and stared at the ceiling. She wasn't angry anymore—not in the loud way. She was just done. The kind of done that came with a quiet sigh and the realization that some people only stay long enough to need you—not love you.

She laid her phone face down and didn't check it again for the rest of the night.

The next day, Micah found her by the vending machines after school. She'd been staring at the selection for five full minutes, trying to decide between sour gummies or peanut M&Ms, and still hadn't moved.

"Decision paralysis?" he asked, sliding up beside her.

She startled, then smiled weakly. "Something like that."

He watched her a moment. "You okay?"

She didn't answer right away. "I'm just tired."

Micah didn't press. "Want a ride home? I'm headed that way."

Leila considered it. She almost said yes. But then her heart flinched with guilt. She wasn't ready for someone to see her like this—not even someone like Micah.

"Nah. I'm good. Thanks, though."

He nodded. "Offer stands."

She finally bought the peanut M&Ms and walked out into the parking lot, her steps slower than usual. The sun was dipping behind the trees, casting long shadows across the pavement. She spotted Destiny's truck a few rows over, Jayla climbing into the passenger side, laughing as she slammed the door shut.

Leila didn't look long.

She turned the other way and walked toward her own car.

The distance between them wasn't just emotional anymore.

It was real. It was physical. It was growing.

And for the first time, Leila wasn't chasing.

That night, Leila didn't bother pretending she was okay.

She skipped her homework, didn't respond to the group chat blowing up with prom plans, and left her dinner plate mostly untouched. Her mom asked if she was feeling sick. She just nodded. It was easier than explaining the kind of sick she actually felt.

The kind of sick where nothing hurt physically, but your chest still ached like you'd run ten miles with an open wound no one could see.

She curled up in bed early, arms around a pillow that didn't hug her back, the lights off, her ceiling fan spinning slow and steady above her. The shadows on her wall danced with every rotation, and for a while, she just stared at them. Counting. Waiting.

For what, she didn't even know anymore.

Maybe for something to change. Maybe for the version of Destiny who used to send late-night texts about stupid memes or impulsive thoughts to suddenly reappear and say, *"Hey. Sorry. I just got scared."*

But that version of Destiny hadn't shown up in weeks. And the one who did exist now? She didn't text back. She laughed with other people. She posted stories with girls like Jayla and smiled in a way that made Leila feel like she'd never mattered.

Leila's phone buzzed on her nightstand, and her heart jumped before she could stop it. Her breath hitched as she reached for it.

Her screen lit up with a message.

Micah.

Still on for tomorrow? I was thinking coffee before we hit the library. My treat.

Leila stared at the message for a long time. The glow of her screen cast pale light on her face, and in that light, she saw herself reflected—eyes tired, mouth tight, heart still halfway somewhere else.

She didn't respond right away.

Instead, her thumb moved back to another message thread.

Destiny's.

She tapped it open.

There it was, just as it had been for days:

Can we talk?

Read.

Still nothing.

No reply. Not even a little gray reaction icon. No dot-dot-dot typing bubble. No soft apology or explanation or even an angry dismissal. Just nothing.

She'd given Destiny space. She hadn't sent follow-ups. She hadn't pushed. She'd waited.

And in return, she got silence.

It wasn't fair. And worse, it wasn't kind.

Leila let the phone drop back onto her chest. Her room felt thick with tension she couldn't name, like her heart was waiting for something to snap. And in that quiet, in the pitch-black space between who they used to be and who they were now, a thought surfaced that scared her more than anything else:

Maybe Destiny doesn't miss me.

Because if she did—wouldn't she have said something?

Wouldn't she have replied?

Wouldn't she have cared enough to stop Leila from unraveling like this?

Leila wiped at her face with the back of her hand, realizing she'd started to cry again—quiet, frustrated tears that slipped down her cheek without ceremony.

She was so tired of this. So tired of being the one who always felt everything too much. So tired of having to pretend she wasn't hurt just because the other person didn't want to deal with the weight of it.

She pulled her covers up higher, wrapping herself tighter, like she could make herself smaller and smaller until she disappeared completely.

The screen of her phone dimmed, then went black.

Somewhere across town, Destiny was probably asleep. Or laughing at some joke. Or holding someone else's hand.

The thought stung so badly she had to sit up.

She grabbed her phone and unlocked it again. For a second, she considered deleting the thread altogether—clearing the conversation, erasing the weight of her unread words.

But she couldn't.

Not yet.

She opened a new message instead. Not to Destiny.

To herself.

She wrote:

I deserved better than this. And I know that. Even if I still wish it had been her.

Then she deleted it.

But it felt good to write it anyway.

She set her phone back down and lay back again, breathing slowly, trying to steady the flood in her chest.

Eventually, exhaustion won. Her body gave up before her mind did.

She drifted off to sleep with her phone tucked under her pillow and the ache of being unfinished tucked inside her ribs.

Somewhere around 3:00 a.m., her phone buzzed.

She didn't wake up.

Not right away.

But when the morning light started to creep through her blinds, she reached for it automatically, eyes squinting against the brightness of the screen.

There it was.

A notification.

Her breath caught.

Destiny.

But it wasn't a message.

It was a story post.

A photo of her and Jayla again. This time in Destiny's bedroom, heads leaned together over a laptop, a big bag of chips between them.

The caption:

"Movie night with the real ones 🖤"

No text reply.

No acknowledgment of the message Leila had poured her last thread of vulnerability into.

Just another moment where she wasn't included. Wasn't chosen.

Wasn't even remembered.

Leila stared at the photo for a long moment, heart cold in her chest.

Then she muted Destiny's account completely.

Not just the stories.

Everything.

Posts. Tags. Mentions.

She wasn't going to watch someone pretend she didn't exist anymore.

Not today.

Maybe not ever again.

Later that morning, as she got dressed, she answered Micah's message.

Yeah. Coffee sounds good.

And it wasn't a replacement.

It wasn't healing.

It was just something.

Something that wasn't nothing.

She brushed her hair in the mirror and whispered to her reflection, "You don't need her to respond to matter."

Her voice shook. But she said it again.

And again.

Until she almost believed it.

As she left the house that day, Destiny didn't cross her mind for the first hour.

And for now, that was enough.

Tomorrow might be different.

But today?

Today, Leila was done waiting.

Chapter 8
The Ones We Pretend Not to Miss

Leila had always imagined the last weeks of senior year would be golden. Something out of a coming-of-age film—sun-drenched afternoons, spontaneous adventures, nostalgia setting in like a warm tide. She thought she'd be walking down the halls smiling at every goodbye, hugging teachers, signing yearbooks, laughing at old inside jokes that used to mean the world.

Instead, everything felt gray.

The sunlight was there, sure—but it felt cold. Like it was shining on someone else's ending. Someone who had it all figured out. Someone who wasn't floating through the days on autopilot.

Each morning felt like climbing out of a pool. Slow. Heavy. Disorienting.

At school, everyone buzzed with excitement. Conversations swirled around her like smoke: *"Did you hear Jamie's going to Stanford?"* *"We should all go to the beach after graduation!"* *"Prom is going to be INSANE."* Leila smiled when she needed to, laughed when someone made a joke nearby, and nodded along like she wasn't drowning quietly inside.

She saw Destiny in the hallways now and then—flashes of her, never more than a glance. Always surrounded by people. Always next to Jayla.

Sometimes Leila would catch her mid-laugh, head tilted back, hand on someone's shoulder like the past six months had never happened. Destiny looked happy. Or at least like someone who knew how to look happy.

Leila wasn't so good at pretending.

Not anymore.

She hadn't heard from Destiny in almost three weeks.

Three weeks of silence. Three weeks of empty space where something used to be. Leila had stopped checking the message thread after the second week. It was like keeping a shrine to a version of someone who no longer existed.

Instead, she turned her focus to survival.

Micah helped.

He never asked too much, never pushed. He was just there— appearing beside her at lunch, sending her TikToks he knew she'd like, occasionally lending her books with his own notes scribbled in the margins. It wasn't romantic. Not yet. Maybe not ever. But it was consistent. And that felt like a miracle in a world where people disappeared the second they got scared.

On Thursday, she sat outside on the senior lawn during free period, watching a group of her classmates rehearse their graduation speeches. A breeze rustled the hem of her hoodie, and she hugged her knees to her chest, tuning out most of the noise.

Micah sat beside her, legs stretched out across the grass.

"You know," he said after a long moment, "you've been doing that thing where your brain goes somewhere else mid-conversation."

She blinked. "Sorry. I didn't realize I was zoning out."

He shrugged. "Didn't say it was bad. Just means you've got a lot going on in there."

Leila gave him a tired half-smile. "Not really. Just... tired of pretending everything's a big deal when it doesn't feel like it."

"Graduation?"

"Everything. People acting like we're never gonna see each other again. That it all meant something. It didn't. Not all of it, anyway."

Micah didn't argue. He leaned back on his elbows and looked at the sky. "Yeah. It's weird how much energy people put into endings when they don't know how to deal with them."

Leila turned to look at him. "That's... oddly insightful for someone who eats three bags of Hot Cheetos a week."

He grinned. "There's wisdom in the spice."

She laughed—really laughed—and for a moment, it felt okay.

But then she saw Destiny.

Across the lawn, she was sitting under a tree with Jayla, earbuds shared between them, a notebook open in Destiny's lap. They looked relaxed. Close. Familiar.

Leila froze.

Her laughter died in her throat.

Micah followed her gaze. "Oh," he said softly.

Leila looked away first. She picked at a loose thread on her jeans, pretending it hadn't punched her in the gut. Pretending it didn't matter.

"Do you ever..." she started, voice quieter now. "Do you ever feel like someone stole the air from the room and didn't even notice?"

Micah didn't answer right away. Then he said, "Yeah. But sometimes I wonder if they noticed and just didn't care."

Leila stared at the grass, jaw tight.

She didn't say anything else.

That night, she stood in her bedroom, holding her graduation robe up to the mirror. The deep navy fabric swayed with the motion of her hands, the gold honor cords looped like tiny nooses across her shoulders. She looked like a ghost version of herself— something polished and distant, someone wearing her own life like a costume.

She took a photo. Not for social media. Just for proof.

Proof that she was still here. Still showing up. Still standing, even if she didn't always want to be.

She almost sent it to Destiny.

She opened the message thread. Typed nothing. Just stared.

Then closed it.

Deleted the photo too.

If Destiny didn't care enough to say anything all this time, then she didn't get to see what came next.

Even if Leila had once imagined her standing next to her—gowns brushing together, fingers maybe brushing too.

Even if she still wanted it.

She set the robe down and lay back on her bed, staring at the ceiling until the shadows made it look like stars. Her heart was tired. Not broken, maybe. But worn down in all the places that used to be soft.

She wasn't sure what she was becoming.

Only that it didn't look anything like what she'd planned.

Graduation day arrived like an apology she didn't ask for.

The sky was a spotless blue, the sun bright and gold and warm—exactly the kind of weather that made people nostalgic in real time. It was the sort of day where people said things like, *"This is it. The beginning of the rest of our lives."* It was the sort of day that made you feel like you were supposed to remember it forever.

Leila wasn't sure she wanted to.

She stood in the crowded field behind the school, navy robe zipped, cap slightly askew, heels sinking into the grass. The buzz of voices surrounded her—friends snapping selfies, parents waving from the stands, teachers hugging students they'd once scolded over tardies.

She spotted her mom in the crowd almost instantly, waving like she was on fire. Leila smiled and waved back, mouthing *"I see you"* before turning her gaze back toward the stage.

Her name would be called in the second row of the Ls. Just enough time to panic, not enough to escape.

As she waited, she glanced around, careful and quick.

Destiny was somewhere on this field. That much she knew. They were graduating together, like they'd always said they would. Same class, same campus, same sky.

But nothing else was the same.

Leila spotted her about twenty feet away, standing in a small group near the edge of the field. Destiny looked beautiful, as always. Her cap was tilted just right, her gold cords swinging with the breeze. Her makeup was subtle but perfect, and her laugh carried even over the buzz of a hundred other conversations.

Jayla stood beside her, of course.

Leila's chest tightened.

She turned her attention back to the stage just in time to catch the principal adjusting the mic and clearing his throat. He launched into a speech filled with tired metaphors and semi-inspiring cliches: *"Write your own stories,"* and *"Chase the unknown,"* and *"Don't let fear stop you from becoming who you're meant to be."*

Leila barely heard any of it.

Instead, she was hearing a memory.

Sophomore year.

Rainy afternoon.

She and Destiny in Leila's bedroom, sprawled across the floor, college brochures spread out like tarot cards. Their fingers brushing as they flipped through pages. Destiny pointing to a flyer from a school upstate and saying, "We could both go here. Roommates. Matching dorm lights. We'd be unstoppable."

And Leila, smiling so wide it hurt, whispering, "I wouldn't want to do it with anyone else."

That memory felt like it had happened in another life.

A ghost of a plan that never survived the storm.

"Leila Jacobs."

Her name snapped her back to the present.

She stepped forward, legs suddenly heavy, walking across the stage toward the principal with a practiced smile that didn't quite reach her eyes. She shook his hand, accepted her diploma, turned to pose for the photo she wouldn't order, then walked back to her seat with applause echoing behind her.

She sat down and exhaled.

Just a few more names. Then freedom. Or something like it.

When the ceremony finally ended, a cheer rose from the crowd. Caps flew in the air, glitter and tassels raining down over the seniors like confetti. Leila didn't throw hers. She didn't even take it off. She just stood, slowly, watching the sky as if hoping it might offer some sort of sign.

She found her mom a few minutes later, wrapped her in a tight hug, and accepted a bouquet of flowers and a thousand compliments she didn't know how to hold.

"You were glowing up there," her mom said, brushing a hair from her face.

Leila smiled weakly. "It's the polyester robe."

Her mom laughed and offered to take pictures. Leila nodded, posing like she was supposed to, arms around classmates, cheeks aching from the weight of all the pretending.

But as the crowd began to thin, something shifted.

She saw Destiny again—alone this time. Just for a moment.

She was walking in Leila's direction, robe flowing, holding her cap in one hand and her phone in the other. Her eyes met Leila's.

And for the first time in weeks, she didn't look away.

Their eyes locked, and the world went still.

The noise, the crowd, the sun—it all dimmed, like a volume knob had been turned down. Destiny's lips parted, just slightly. Her steps slowed.

For half a second, Leila thought she was going to walk over.

Say something.

Anything.

But then Jayla called her name from across the field. Destiny hesitated. Turned her head.

And just like that, she veered away.

Leila watched her go.

It didn't feel like heartbreak. It felt like confirmation.

That this was the new reality.

That whatever they'd been—whatever it might have become— was buried now, beneath all the words they never said.

Later, in the car on the way home, Leila stared out the window, the flowers from her mom wilting slightly in her lap.

"You okay, honey?" her mom asked gently.

"Yeah," Leila said, nodding.

But her voice cracked.

And her mom didn't ask again.

Summer crept in quietly, without ceremony or welcome.

One day Leila was standing in a sea of navy robes on the football field, and the next, she was lying in bed at noon, watching dust dance in the sunlight. The air was thick and slow, and so were her thoughts. Her alarm clock remained off. Her phone buzzed less. Time blurred, unstructured, unstopped.

This wasn't the summer she and Destiny had talked about.

They used to plan it in whispers during math class. Beach trips. Coffee shop crawls. One last sleepover where they'd stay up all night watching dumb movies and drinking soda until they crashed side-by-side. They were going to make it *their* summer.

Now, it felt like someone else's story entirely.

Leila tried not to think about it, but the quiet made it hard not to.

Micah texted more often now. They weren't close-close, not like she and Destiny had been, but they had a rhythm. He sent her playlists and poems. She sent him pictures of the sky or dumb memes she thought he'd like. It was low pressure. A lifeline disguised as a friendship.

On a humid Friday evening, he invited her to a poetry night at a small café downtown. "You need to get out of the house," he said. "And you love words, don't pretend you don't."

She almost said no.

But something in her—something tired of lying in bed—said yes.

So she put on a sundress that didn't feel like hers and left the house before she could change her mind.

The café was cozy, dimly lit with string lights and flickering candles. The scent of lavender and old books hung in the air. Leila had never been there before, but it felt familiar somehow—like a place she would've brought Destiny.

Micah greeted her with a smile and a cup of chai. "You showed," he said, mock-surprised.

"Barely," Leila replied, sipping it gratefully. "Is this bribery?"

"Absolutely."

They sat at a corner table near the back, and as the first performer took the mic, Leila tried to let herself be present. The words flowed—some soft and hesitant, others loud and angry, like purges disguised as poetry. She liked the honesty of it all. No one here was pretending to be okay. That alone made her breathe easier.

Halfway through the night, Micah leaned close and whispered, "You'd kill it up there."

Leila snorted. "I'd combust."

"I mean it," he said. "You write like someone who knows things."

Leila blinked. Her chest tightened—not in a bad way, but in that unfamiliar way kindness sometimes did when you weren't used to receiving it.

"I used to," she murmured. "Before everything."

Micah didn't ask what "everything" meant. He just nodded.

Later, someone snapped a photo of them at the table—heads tilted toward each other, mid-laugh. Leila didn't even know it had happened until she got home and saw the tag.

She hesitated for a long moment before clicking "add to story."

The comments came quickly: hearts, compliments, jokes.

But it was the view count that got her.

Because Destiny saw it.

She hadn't messaged. Of course not. But her name sat there, clear as day, under "seen by."

And that did something weird to Leila's chest.

Not pain. Not longing.

Anger.

Not the burning kind, but the dull, resigned kind. The kind that came from knowing someone was still watching—but not caring enough to do anything about it.

That night, Destiny posted a photo on her story too. Just a selfie. Slightly filtered. Wearing a cozy hoodie, smiling faintly into the camera.

The caption read:

Finally healing.

Leila stared at it for a long time. Then she turned her phone off.

Later that night, curled on the couch with her laptop open but untouched, Leila whispered aloud, "Then why do I still feel broken?"

No one answered.

She didn't expect them to.

The next day, her mom found her in the kitchen, staring at the same sentence in her journal she'd been trying to finish for twenty minutes.

"You okay, baby?" she asked, pouring coffee.

Leila didn't look up. "Do you ever feel like... like someone left, and you don't get to be mad because they didn't technically do anything wrong?"

Her mom paused. Then sat down across from her.

"I think," she said gently, "that some of the worst heartbreaks are the ones no one else sees. The ones you can't explain because there's no big fight, no betrayal. Just... absence."

Leila swallowed.

Her mom reached across the table, covering her hand.

"And just because someone walks away quietly doesn't mean it didn't hurt. Or that you're not allowed to miss them."

"I don't want to miss her," Leila whispered.

"I know."

They sat like that for a while—no solutions, no conclusions. Just presence.

And maybe that was enough, for now.

The days bled together after that.

Long afternoons where the heat clung to Leila's skin and everything felt sticky, unresolved. She read books but didn't finish them. Listened to music but skipped most of the songs halfway through. She started writing again, only to scratch out every line before it could mean anything.

The ache hadn't gone away—it had just gotten quieter. Quieter, but deeper. Like it had settled into her bones, no longer a sharp pain but a dull, constant weight.

And still, no message from Destiny.

Leila hadn't expected one—not really—but some part of her had hoped. Graduation had come and gone. Summer had started.

Their story, whatever it was, felt stuck in a drawer neither of them knew how to open again.

And yet...

Late one night, as Leila scrolled through her camera roll, she saw it again—*the photo.* The one she took the night they held hands on the couch. Destiny's head was resting on her shoulder. Their hands, intertwined. The edges of their faces barely visible in the dim light of the TV glow. She had taken it without thinking. A quiet moment. A forever kind of moment.

She stared at it until her eyes stung.

Then, without letting herself hesitate, she opened their message thread.

Still no new texts. Still nothing since *"Can we talk?"*

But she began typing.

Do you ever think about that night?

She paused. Deleted it.

I don't even know where we went wrong. Or if we were ever even going right.

Deleted.

I wish we'd said more. I wish we hadn't stopped when it mattered.

Deleted.

She closed the thread and set her phone down with trembling hands.

Across town, Destiny lay in bed, her phone screen glowing softly in the dark.

She had Leila's messages bookmarked. Not out loud—not in the app. But in her mind. She knew exactly what they said. Knew how long they'd been sitting there, unread. Knew what she wanted to say back, but not how to say it.

She opened their conversation for the first time in days.

Scrolled to the top.

To the start.

Messages from months ago. Dumb memes. Homework questions. That weird night when Destiny had confessed she hated thunderstorms, and Leila had immediately sent her a voice note reading a poem to distract her.

A smile tugged at Destiny's lips.

She typed.

I miss—

Backspaced.

Typed again.

Are you—

Backspaced.

She closed her eyes and let her fingers hover over the keyboard. The words were there. She just couldn't get them out. Because what if Leila had moved on? What if Micah was more than just a friend now? What if Destiny had waited too long, stayed quiet too long?

She clicked on Leila's story out of habit.

There she was, sitting on a picnic blanket, hair curled around her face, laughing at something someone had said behind the camera. A cup of iced coffee in one hand. The golden-hour sun kissed her skin, and for a second, Destiny forgot how to breathe.

She tapped through to the next slide.

Micah. Sitting beside Leila. Holding a copy of some indie poetry zine. His head leaned toward hers. Their smiles looked like a secret.

Destiny stared at it too long.

Typed again.

You look happy.

Deleted.

Instead, she did something she hadn't done in weeks.

She hovered over Leila's name.

Typing...

Leila saw it almost immediately. The notification lit up at the top of her screen, and her stomach flipped like a rollercoaster had dropped beneath her.

Destiny was typing.

She stared at the screen, heart pounding, frozen in place.

But then—

Nothing.

No message came through.

The dots vanished.

Leila waited. Refreshed the chat. Nothing.

She bit the inside of her cheek, pulse still racing.

Why won't she just say it? she thought. *Why does she keep doing this—almost reaching out, then pulling away?*

Part of her wanted to send a message first. To break the silence once and for all. But she didn't want to beg. Not again. Not after how hard it had been to hold back the first time.

Instead, she opened her Notes app and started typing what she couldn't say aloud.

We could've been something real. You know that, right? We were more than just "almost." You looked at me like I was yours. And I—

She stopped typing.

She didn't delete it.

But she didn't send it either.

The next day, Destiny sat in her car outside a smoothie shop, engine off, AC on. Her phone buzzed with a text from Jayla: *Coming?*

She stared at it but didn't reply. Instead, she opened her camera roll and stared at the photo from the couch—the one Leila didn't know she had taken. She had it, too. That night mattered to both of them.

She knew it wasn't just in her head.

But maybe... maybe it was too late now.

She opened Leila's thread again.

Still nothing new.

She almost sent a voice note. Just hit record and said, *"I'm sorry. I miss you. Can we try again?"*

But she didn't.

Because fear had a way of sounding logical.

She turned off her phone and walked into the smoothie shop, leaving Leila's name glowing behind her on the screen.

Somewhere, that message still lived—in a thought, a pause, a silence.

And for now, silence would win.

Chapter 9
When Silence Starts to Scream

Leila didn't mean to snap at her mom.

It just... happened. One minute, her mom was gently suggesting she start packing for college— *"Just a box or two, baby, it'll feel good to get ahead"*—and the next, Leila was slamming her bedroom door and yelling, "I said I'll do it later!"

The silence that followed was heavier than the words themselves.

Leila stood frozen in her room, hands clenched into fists at her sides, breathing hard. Her mom hadn't deserved that. She knew that. But the pressure had been building for weeks now— tightening around her ribs, humming beneath her skin like static.

She hadn't meant to explode.

But she had.

And once the quiet returned, it was worse.

She sat down on the floor, legs crossed, back against her bed frame, and let herself feel everything she'd been trying so hard to outrun. It wasn't just about college. Or packing. Or any of it.

It was about Destiny.

Always about Destiny.

It was the fact that every time her phone buzzed, a piece of her still hoped it would be her.

It was the fact that she'd gone entire days pretending she didn't care, only to lie awake at night, staring at the ceiling, whispering, *"Why did you let me go?"*

It was the fact that even now, weeks later, she couldn't throw away the hoodie Destiny left at her house last fall. It still hung on the back of her chair, like it was waiting for someone to claim it.

Leila reached up and tugged it into her lap.

She buried her face in it.

It didn't smell like Destiny anymore. Just dust and time. But the shape of it still remembered her. The sleeves still folded the same way Destiny always wore them—pushed halfway up, thumb poking through a worn-out hole near the cuff.

She clutched the fabric tighter.

"I hate this," she said aloud. Her voice cracked.

She stood abruptly, needing to move, needing to do something. She yanked open her desk drawer, the one full of old birthday cards and notes and things she couldn't throw away. She didn't even know what she was looking for.

But then she saw it.

A tiny, crumpled piece of paper, folded into a triangle. Her name scribbled on the outside in looping letters.

It was a note Destiny had passed her during junior year English. Leila had forgotten it even existed. Her hands shook as she unfolded it.

Leilaaaa. If we have to read one more metaphor about birds flying free I'm gonna fly out the window. You down for waffles after school? You're my favorite human. Forever friends. No take backs.

—D.

Leila sat on the edge of her bed and read it three more times.

Then whispered, "Liar."

It wasn't fair. She knew Destiny probably hadn't meant to be cruel. But still—*forever friends*? Where was forever now? Where was all the care she'd sworn she had?

Where was the girl who had cried in her arms on a rainy night and held her hand like it meant something?

Where was the honesty?

Leila grabbed her phone and opened Destiny's thread.

Still nothing new.

Still the same silence that had stretched on for months now. The same unanswered question. The same unread truths.

She started typing.

Do you even miss me?

Backspaced.

I've been trying to move on. But I can't. Not really. You were more than just my best friend. I think you knew that.

Deleted.

Her thumb hovered over the keyboard.

She thought about what she really wanted.

Not even to get Destiny back.

Just the truth.

Just a *why*.

She typed again.

I found your note today. The one that said 'forever friends.' I believed you. I think that's what hurts the most.

She stared at the message.

Her heart pounded.

But she didn't hit send.

Instead, she saved it as a draft and threw the phone across her bed like it burned.

Her breath was shaky. Her vision blurred.

This wasn't just longing anymore. It was grief.

Real, quiet, intimate grief.

Because there's a kind of heartbreak that comes from watching someone fall out of love with you—but the one Leila felt was deeper.

It came from watching someone erase you without saying goodbye.

That night, she didn't eat dinner.

She didn't respond to Micah's check-in text. He meant well, but she didn't have the energy to pretend she wasn't still haunted.

She turned off her phone. Dimmed the lights.

Sat in silence.

Eventually, she reached for her journal. The one she hadn't touched in weeks.

She didn't write poetry.

She didn't even write prose.

She just wrote her name.

Leila. Leila. Leila.

Over and over, until the page was full.

Like she needed to remind herself that she was still here.

That she existed, even if Destiny wasn't looking anymore.

Jayla wasn't stupid.

People often mistook her calm for cluelessness, like being chill meant she didn't pay attention. But Jayla noticed everything—especially when it came to Destiny.

She'd seen the way Destiny looked at her phone when she thought no one was watching.

The way she scrolled through Instagram, paused too long on one specific story, and quickly turned the screen face-down. She knew that name. Everyone at school did. Leila Jacobs. Destiny's best friend turned ghost turned question mark.

Jayla hadn't asked. Not directly. She wasn't the confrontational type. But she didn't need to ask to know something had happened between them—something big.

Something that still haunted Destiny.

It was the way Destiny pulled her sleeves down over her hands when she was nervous. The way she'd get quiet in the middle of conversations. The way her laugh dimmed when someone mentioned college, or poetry, or anything that might remind her of the girl who used to make her mixtapes and annotate her favorite books.

Jayla had tried to be patient.

She liked Destiny. Genuinely. They'd become friends after soccer season ended last fall—late practices and bus rides turning into coffee meetups and shared playlists. There was something easy about them. Low-maintenance. They never had to over-explain themselves. It was refreshing.

But the more time passed, the more Jayla realized Destiny wasn't fully present—not with her, not really.

She was somewhere else.

Still caught up in something unfinished.

Something that had left fingerprints on her, even now.

One evening in mid-July, they were sitting on Jayla's porch, drinking lemon tea and watching the sky turn orange. Destiny was scrolling through her phone again, bottom lip caught between her teeth. Her thumb hovered over the screen for so long that Jayla leaned over and asked, "You gonna text her or just stare at the bubble?"

Destiny startled.

Jayla raised an eyebrow. "Sorry. I mean... you're not exactly subtle."

Destiny hesitated, then handed her the phone without saying a word.

It was open to Leila's profile. A muted story glowing around her name. The picture: Leila, smiling with some boy under a tree. A book open between them. The caption read: *Summer's softest pages.*

Jayla blinked. "Is this the guy she's seeing?"

"I don't know," Destiny said quietly. "I don't think so. I mean, maybe. I haven't... I haven't talked to her."

Jayla handed the phone back. "You could."

Destiny let out a soft laugh, but it was bitter. "What would I even say? 'Sorry I disappeared after letting you hold all my secrets in your hands'? 'Sorry I didn't know what to do with what we were'? I hurt her."

Jayla tilted her head. "You still care?"

Destiny's voice dropped. "I never stopped."

The air between them thickened. Jayla took a long sip of her tea, letting the silence settle before she spoke again.

"You know... you never really talked about what she was to you. Like, *really* was."

Destiny gave a small nod. "She was... she is... the only person who ever made me feel like I wasn't broken."

Jayla didn't flinch at that.

She just nodded, lips pressed together, eyes on the horizon.

"Then why'd you leave?"

Destiny looked down. "Because I was scared. Because I didn't know if she felt the same way, or if I was making it all up in my head. Because she was becoming something I didn't have a name for and I couldn't stand the thought of saying it and being wrong."

Jayla set her mug down. "You weren't wrong."

Destiny looked up.

Jayla gave her a small smile—soft, but knowing. "You should've seen how she looked at you. Even when you weren't looking back."

Destiny blinked, eyes glassy.

Jayla shrugged. "You don't have to explain yourself to me, but don't lie to yourself either. You're not over her. And I don't think you'll forgive yourself if you don't try."

Destiny stayed quiet for a long time. Then said, "I think I broke us."

Jayla's voice was gentle. "Then fix it."

A beat of silence. Then another.

Finally, Destiny whispered, "Why are you being so cool about this?"

Jayla chuckled. "Because I've been the Leila before. It sucks when someone leaves you wondering."

Destiny swallowed hard.

Jayla leaned back against the porch railing, eyes drifting to the stars beginning to blink into view. "Besides, I'd rather lose you to the truth than keep you in something fake."

Destiny nodded, barely breathing.

That night, after she got home, she stared at her phone for over an hour.

She opened Leila's thread.

Typed:

Can I talk to you?

Deleted it.

Typed again:

I miss you. I'm sorry. I should've never left things the way I did.

Deleted.

Her hands trembled.

She opened her camera roll. Found the photo again—the one from the night they held hands on the couch. The one that still made her heart ache.

She stared at it until her eyes burned.

Then, slowly, she put her phone down and picked up her journal.

She didn't know what she was going to write.

But she knew she had to start.

Leila hadn't planned on going to the café.

She just needed air. A reason to leave the house that wasn't about moving boxes or pretending to be excited about orientation emails. The café on Main was one of the only places in town that still felt neutral—where the chairs were mismatched and the music was soft and the baristas didn't ask questions.

She brought her journal and a book she wasn't actually reading. She ordered a lavender iced tea, settled into her usual corner booth, and tried not to check her phone. Her draft to Destiny still sat unsent. Her chest still burned with everything she hadn't said.

She was halfway through scribbling something—anything—in the margins of her notebook when the bell above the café door rang.

She didn't look up at first.

Until she heard the voice.

Familiar.

Soft.

"I'll just grab a tea," Destiny was saying to the barista, voice low but audible.

Leila froze.

Her pen slipped.

She lifted her eyes just in time to see her.

Destiny.

Hair braided down one side, wearing a navy t-shirt and black jeans. No makeup. No smile. A little older somehow.

A little more tired.

And not alone.

A girl stood next to her—Destiny's cousin, maybe. Someone Leila didn't recognize. But they were talking easily, like this was just an errand. Like this wasn't the first time Destiny had been in the same room as Leila in over two months.

Leila's pulse thundered in her ears.

She looked down quickly, back at her notebook, hoping—somehow, stupidly—that Destiny hadn't seen her.

But she had.

Leila felt it.

The shift in the air. The hesitation in Destiny's breath. That split-second pause that said *I see you too.*

For a moment, neither of them moved.

Then the girl beside Destiny said something and walked toward the pickup counter.

Destiny stood still.

Then, slowly, she walked over to Leila's table.

Leila didn't look up at first.

Not until Destiny said, "Hey."

She looked up.

And everything stopped.

For a second, all Leila could see was that night on the couch. The way Destiny's fingers had curled around hers. The sound of her voice, fragile and shaking. The weight of her body pressed into her side. It hit her like a punch to the ribs.

"What do you want?" Leila asked, voice flat.

Destiny flinched, but didn't back away. "Can I sit?"

Leila didn't answer.

But she didn't say no, either.

Destiny sat.

The silence between them stretched.

Finally, Destiny said, "I didn't expect to see you."

Leila let out a hollow laugh. "Right. Because you weren't checking my stories or anything."

Destiny's cheeks flushed. "I was just—"

"Don't," Leila said sharply. "Don't lie."

Destiny's mouth snapped shut.

Another silence.

The café felt too quiet, like everyone else had disappeared.

Leila stared at her, eyes hard. "You don't get to pretend this is normal."

"I'm not," Destiny said quickly. "I'm not pretending."

"Then what are you doing here?" Leila snapped. "Checking to see if I'm still broken enough to wait for you?"

Destiny's eyes widened. "That's not fair."

"No," Leila said, voice rising. "What's not fair is the way you vanished. The way you made me feel like I was crazy for thinking we meant something—when you *knew* we did."

"I never said we didn't—"

"But you acted like it!" Leila shot back. "You acted like that night meant nothing. Like I was just... just someone to hold onto when it was convenient."

"I was scared," Destiny said, almost whispering.

Leila stared at her. "Of what? Of me?"

"Of *us.* Of what I was feeling," Destiny said, her voice cracking now. "I didn't know what it meant. I didn't know if you felt it too, or if I was reading too much into things."

"You were *not* reading too much into it," Leila said, tears brimming. "You don't cry into someone's arms and hold their hand for hours and make them feel like they're safe and seen and *wanted*—and then pretend none of it mattered."

Destiny swallowed hard. "I never pretended it didn't matter."

"You just didn't care enough to stay."

"That's not true."

"Then *why didn't you talk to me?!*" Leila's voice cracked, loud enough that a barista glanced over from the counter. "I was right there, Destiny. I was *waiting.* I sent you message after message and you read them and said nothing. Nothing."

Destiny's eyes welled. "Because I didn't know how to explain what I was feeling. Because I didn't want to hurt you more by saying the wrong thing."

"You know what hurts more than the wrong thing?" Leila whispered. "Saying nothing."

That landed like a stone between them.

Neither of them spoke for a long moment.

Destiny wiped her eyes. "I thought maybe if I disappeared, you'd forget me. Move on. Be okay."

"You don't get to decide that for me," Leila said quietly. "You don't get to break my heart and then disappear like I should thank you for leaving."

Destiny looked down, guilt etched into every line of her face. "I'm sorry," she whispered.

"I know," Leila said. "But I don't know if that's enough."

Destiny nodded slowly. "I just wanted to say it."

She stood up then, like the moment had passed.

Her tea order was probably ready.

Her cousin was probably waiting.

This wasn't the reunion either of them had imagined.

It wasn't closure, either.

It was just... an earthquake.

A necessary break.

As Destiny turned to leave, she paused.

"I did love you," she said, so softly Leila almost didn't catch it.

Then she walked away.

And Leila just sat there.

Staring at her notebook.

Hands shaking.

Heart breaking all over again.

Leila didn't go home right away.

She sat in her car in the café parking lot for almost an hour, the engine off, windows fogged with heat and grief. She wasn't crying, not exactly. The tears had stopped halfway through the argument. What was left now wasn't loud or cinematic.

It was quieter.

Worse.

She kept replaying the moment in her head, over and over—the way Destiny's voice had cracked when she said *I did love you*, like it was both a confession and a goodbye.

Had.

Past tense.

It echoed.

The words didn't feel like healing. They felt like salt rubbed into the cracks.

Because if she had loved her, why hadn't she stayed? Why hadn't she replied? Why had she let Leila sit in the wreckage for months without saying a word?

Love didn't look like that.

Did it?

Leila pressed her forehead against the steering wheel and let out a breath that shook. Her chest felt like a drawer that had been forced open and then left that way—contents spilled, nothing put back in place.

Honesty was supposed to fix things.

But right now, it just made her feel exposed.

Later that night, her mom knocked softly on her door.

"Want some tea?"

Leila didn't answer right away.

"Chamomile," her mom added. "Extra honey."

Leila finally opened the door and nodded.

They sat in the living room with the TV on mute, the lights low. Leila's mug sat untouched in her lap.

Her mom didn't press. She just waited.

Finally, Leila said, "I saw her today."

Her mom nodded, as if she already knew.

"I thought I'd feel better if we talked," Leila said, voice quiet. "I thought maybe I'd get some kind of closure. But it just made everything worse."

"What happened?"

"We fought. I said things I didn't mean, and she said things I think she meant too much."

Her mom set down her tea. "And how do you feel?"

"I feel like..." Leila stared at her hands. "I feel like I lost something I never even got to name."

There it was.

The truth, in its rawest form.

Her mom didn't flinch. "Do you think you loved her?"

Leila's throat tightened. "I don't know. Maybe."

Pause.

"Yes."

Her mom reached over and gently took her hand. "Then you're grieving something real. It doesn't have to be defined to matter."

Leila didn't cry.

But something in her shifted.

Across town, Destiny sat on her bedroom floor, her back against her bed, her laptop open to an old playlist Leila had made for her sophomore year. The title was a dumb inside joke—something about frogs and galaxies—and the cover photo was a blurry picture of the two of them from a sleepover.

She hit play.

The first song started, and she almost turned it off.

But she didn't.

She needed to feel it.

Needed to stop running.

The fight at the café had cracked something open in her. Something she'd boarded up months ago, hoping it would disappear if she just ignored it long enough.

But seeing Leila again—hearing the anger in her voice, the heartbreak in her words—had reminded Destiny that silence wasn't the same as healing. She'd thought she was protecting them both by disappearing.

But maybe she'd just been protecting herself from having to say things she didn't understand.

Her phone buzzed on the floor next to her.

It was Jayla.

You okay?

Destiny didn't answer. Not yet.

Instead, she opened the drawer of her nightstand and pulled out a small notebook. One she hadn't touched since spring. The cover was purple and slightly bent, the spine cracking from use.

Inside, the margins were full of Leila's name.

Sometimes written neatly. Sometimes scribbled in loops. Sometimes surrounded by tiny stars or lyrics or question marks.

She flipped to the last page she'd written.

A poem. Unfinished.
She added a line.
Then another.
Then stopped.
She opened her Notes app. Scrolled to a draft she'd started weeks ago—a message she'd never sent.

I think I was in love with you before I knew what that meant. I think I still am, in a way. Even if it's messy. Even if I don't deserve to say it now.

She re-read it.
Didn't delete it.
But didn't send it, either.
Instead, she whispered into the quiet, "I wish I'd said it sooner."

The next morning, Leila woke up earlier than usual. The sun was barely up. Her room was filled with a soft orange light that made everything feel gentler than it had the night before.

She sat on her bed and stared at the unsent message to Destiny.

I found your note today. The one that said "forever friends." I believed you. I think that's what hurts the most.

She tapped the screen.
Then added:

I think I loved you, too. And I wish we'd figured it out before we broke it.

Her finger hovered over the send button.
Her chest tightened.
And then—
She didn't send it.
Instead, she hit **Save as Draft.**
Just like that.
She wasn't ready.
Not yet.
But she wasn't pretending anymore, either.
And maybe that was enough.
For now.

The last Saturday before college felt nothing like Leila thought it would.

The sun was out. Her suitcase sat open at the foot of her bed. A stack of clean notebooks waited to be packed beside a roll of new pens. Her mom had made pancakes. Her acceptance letter was still pinned on the fridge like a badge of honor.

Everything on the outside looked bright.

But Leila sat cross-legged on the floor, staring at her phone like it was a ticking bomb.

The draft was still there.

The message she'd written after the fight at the café. Raw, honest, heavy.

I found your note today. The one that said "forever friends." I believed you. I think that's what hurts the most.

I think I loved you, too. And I wish we'd figured it out before we broke it.

She'd read it ten times since writing it. Each time, her heart beat faster. Each time, her thumb hovered over the send button. And each time, she'd chickened out.

Because what came after?

What if Destiny didn't respond? Or worse—what if she did, but it wasn't what Leila wanted to hear?

What if she says she's moved on? What if she says she loved me once, but not anymore?

The truth had never scared her so much.

She stood up and began folding clothes into her suitcase to distract herself. Each shirt, each pair of jeans, felt like a countdown. She was leaving. This town, these streets, this silence—it would all be behind her soon.

But Destiny would still be here.

That thought stung more than it should have.

When she got to the hoodie—*Destiny's* hoodie—she paused.

It was still soft. Still smelled faintly of something like nostalgia.

Leila folded it carefully. Set it on top of her things. And kept packing.

On the other side of town, Destiny sat on the edge of her bed, suitcase open, heart full.

She hadn't written Leila back after the fight. Not because she didn't care. Because she cared *too* much.

The message draft sat in her notes, waiting, like a held breath.

I'm sorry I let fear make me disappear. I wanted to be yours. I just didn't know how to say it back then.

I still don't know what we were, but I know I loved you. I still do.

Is it too late to say that?

She read it twice.

Her hands were cold.

Jayla had stopped texting a few days ago. Not in a passive-aggressive way. Just... quietly. Like she was giving Destiny space to figure it out. Like she knew Destiny needed to be alone with this one.

Destiny hated how long it had taken her to find the words. Hated how long she had let silence stand in for honesty.

But writing the message had been easy.

Sending it?

That was another thing entirely.

What if Leila didn't want to hear it?

What if she'd closed that door already?

What if the boy in the picnic photos wasn't just a friend anymore?

Destiny stared at her phone, chewing the inside of her cheek.

Then, slowly, she typed one more line.

If you still want to know the truth... I'll tell you everything.

She took a breath.

Her finger hovered over **Send.**

But she didn't move.

The seconds passed like hours.

And then—

She closed the message.

Saved as draft.

That evening, Leila stood in her bedroom doorway, scanning

the space like she was saying goodbye to something more than just four walls. Her suitcase was zipped. Her shelves empty. Her lamp unplugged.

She sat on the bed, picked up her phone again.

The message waited for her.

It looked so small on the screen. Just a few sentences.

But it held everything she hadn't been brave enough to say out loud.

She thought about the way Destiny had looked at her in the café.

The way her voice broke when she said, *I did love you.*

The way she didn't try to take it back.

Leila took a shaky breath.

She clicked into the message. Reread every word.

Her thumb hovered.

Pressed.

And then—

Backed out.

Saved as draft.

She let her phone fall beside her on the bed.

Maybe this was what they were now.

Drafts.

Half-written things.

Almosts.

But not quite.

Destiny sat in her car the next morning, parked in front of a gas station on the way to her aunt's place. Her mom had asked her to drop something off—something about storage boxes and goodbyes—but Destiny wasn't really listening.

She was staring at her phone.

Her hands were shaking again.

She opened Leila's Instagram. Saw her latest post: a photo of a sunset. No people in it. Just soft orange clouds and the caption:

Packing up. Starting over. Whatever that means.

Destiny almost replied.

Almost said, *I'm still here, if you want me.*

But she didn't.

Instead, she whispered, "I hope you find peace, even if it's not with me."

Then she put her phone down, started the engine, and drove away.

Leila woke up early the morning of her move.

She showered, dressed, and stood in front of her mirror one last time. Her room looked foreign now—bare walls, empty drawers, the faint outline of old posters still visible like ghosts.

She grabbed her phone and opened her drafts.

Destiny's message sat there like it always had.

Waiting.

Hopeful.

She didn't delete it.

But she didn't send it, either.

Instead, she whispered, "You know where to find me."

Then she slid the phone into her bag, zipped it up, and walked downstairs.

She didn't look back.

Not yet.

Chapter 10
A New Dawn

The thing about starting over, Leila had learned, was that it didn't really feel like starting over. It felt more like slipping into a river that had already been running, trying to match its current before it dragged you under.

Her first week of college blurred like a dream: too many names, too many syllabi, too many new buildings to get lost in. People talked fast and smiled big. Everyone seemed desperate to reinvent themselves—sharper, cooler, freer than who they'd been in high school. Leila wasn't sure who she was trying to be yet.

Maybe someone who didn't flinch when she heard Destiny's name in her thoughts.

Maybe someone who didn't reach for her phone every time something beautiful happened.

Her roommate, Candace, was chatty and sweet and already obsessed with a TA in their intro psych class. Their floor was loud with music and laughter every night. She liked it, even if she wasn't sure how to belong in it yet. There was freedom in anonymity, she told herself. A clean slate.

But freedom, it turned out, had a sharp edge.

And it found her on a Tuesday morning.

Leila was late to her second seminar of the day— *"Memory, Identity, and the Written Word."* It was a small, discussion-based class, one she'd picked because she thought it would make her fall in love with literature again.

She hadn't expected it to make her feel like she'd been punched in the chest.

She walked in five minutes after the professor, head down, bag sliding off her shoulder. The room was bright, bookshelves lining the walls, a round table instead of desks. Twelve students total. Intimate. Unforgiving.

She scanned the seats, looking for a free spot—

—and froze.

Destiny.

Sitting on the far side of the circle, notebook open, hair in a loose braid, fingers tapping softly against the table.

Their eyes met.

It was instant.

Shock. Then disbelief. Then something else. Something electric.

Leila's stomach dropped.

The professor—an older woman with silver curls and too many bracelets—cleared her throat. "You must be Leila. Welcome. There's a seat next to Destiny."

Of course there was.

Leila's feet moved before her brain caught up. She slid into the seat slowly, heart slamming. Destiny didn't say anything. Just looked straight ahead, posture too perfect, jaw tight.

Leila sat stiffly beside her, leaving just enough space between their chairs to feel like a canyon.

This wasn't happening.

It couldn't be.

She hadn't seen Destiny in over two months. Not in person. Not like this. Just fragments—photos, memories, unsent messages. And now here she was, real and alive and sitting six inches away.

The professor began to speak, but Leila barely heard her.

Something about identity through literature, how storytelling connects personal memory to collective truth. Leila stared at the syllabus in front of her, words swimming.

Out of the corner of her eye, Destiny shifted.

Not a flinch. Just a tiny inhale.

Leila hadn't even thought they might end up at the same school. She'd chosen this place because it felt big and far away. She hadn't checked where Destiny was going. She'd told herself it didn't matter.

Apparently, it did.

"I'll be dividing you into semester-long project groups," the professor was saying now. "You'll create a collaborative piece—something that captures your personal memory through collective storytelling. It will be a mix of writing, performance, and curation. Pairs or trios."

Leila's stomach twisted.

She already knew.

She didn't know how, but she knew.

The professor started reading names.

"Leila Jacobs... Destiny Moore..."

No.

"...and Tyrese Alston. You three will be group two."

Leila didn't breathe.

Destiny didn't move.

Tyrese, a tall guy with thick glasses and a kind smile, glanced between them and gave a little shrug. "Cool," he said. "Nice to meet you both."

Leila forced herself to nod.

The rest of the names blurred. Her palms were sweating. She could feel Destiny beside her—still, silent, tense. Not once did she turn. Not once did she speak.

When class ended, chairs scraped and people laughed as they filed out. Leila stayed seated for a second too long, unsure if her legs would work.

Destiny stood.

Gathered her things.

Turned slightly.

Their eyes met again.

This time, there was something else there. Not surprise. Not fear.

Longing.

But still—no words.

Destiny broke eye contact first.

And then she left.

Leila sat frozen for a few more seconds.

Then slowly packed up her things and walked out into the sunlight, blinking like she hadn't seen daylight in weeks.

She walked back to her dorm in silence.

Didn't play music. Didn't text anyone.

That night, she lay in bed staring at the ceiling, wondering how the world could fold in on itself like that—how it could bring you face to face with everything you'd spent the summer trying to forget.

Because she'd been trying. God, she had tried.

But seeing Destiny again had shattered every piece of pretending she'd carefully arranged.

She still loved her.

She never stopped.

And now, they were in the same class, the same group, the same orbit again.

The universe, apparently, didn't believe in clean breaks.

The first group meeting was three days later.

The seminar professor had told them to find time outside of class to start brainstorming their "collaborative memory project"—whatever that meant. Tyrese set up a group chat right away, naming it *Memory Makers* with a winking emoji, and suggested meeting at the campus library on Saturday afternoon.

Leila typed *Sounds good!* before she could think too hard.

Destiny responded with a thumbs-up.

It was the first digital proof she'd existed in Leila's life in over two months.

And it hurt more than it helped.

Saturday came too fast.

Leila arrived early, heart in her throat, fingers already tingling from overthinking everything. She'd tied her hair up, kept her outfit casual. She told herself it didn't matter what she looked like. She told herself a thousand things.

None of them stopped the shaking in her hands.

The library study room was small, windowed on three sides, filled with afternoon light and the low hum of central air. She picked the seat farthest from the door and opened her laptop, pretending to be deep in a document that didn't exist yet.

Tyrese showed up next, wearing a hoodie that said *Writer-ish* and carrying a bag of chips. "Hope y'all don't mind me snacking," he said with a grin, dropping into the seat next to her.

She smiled. "I'm good."

And then—Destiny.

She walked in quietly, her notebook already open, pen tucked behind her ear. She wore a denim jacket Leila had seen before. Once. Last spring. On the night they sat too close on the couch and said nothing about how badly they wanted to say something.

Leila's breath hitched.

"Hey," Destiny said, nodding at them both. Her voice was polite. Careful.

"Hey," Tyrese replied easily. "Alright, creatives—let's figure this thing out."

They started outlining ideas. Something about storytelling through objects. A photo album with poems. An audio collage of voices. Tyrese had no shortage of suggestions, tossing them out between handfuls of chips and bad puns.

Leila contributed. So did Destiny.

But never to each other.

Their words curved around the room, never colliding. Leila would say something, and Destiny would nod without looking up. Destiny would offer a note, and Leila would scribble it down without speaking.

To anyone else, it probably looked normal.

To Leila, it felt like walking across glass barefoot.

The silence wasn't cold. It was worse—it was restrained. It was watching someone you used to breathe beside now measure every exhale.

At one point, Tyrese leaned back and said, "So... did you two go to the same high school or something? You seem like you kinda know each other."

The question shattered the surface.

Leila's pen stilled.

Destiny blinked.

Then smiled—tight, practiced. "Yeah. Sort of."

Leila forced a nod. "It's a small world."

Tyrese laughed. "Bet there's a story there."

Neither of them answered.

He moved on, thankfully, diving back into the brainstorming with the kind of ease Leila envied.

Eventually, they broke for the day, agreeing to each draft a short piece inspired by a childhood object and bring it to the next meeting. Tyrese left first, waving over his shoulder.

Destiny lingered a second longer.

Leila felt it—the pull in the air.

But Destiny didn't say anything.

She just walked out.

Leila stayed behind.

Alone again.

The next few meetings followed the same pattern. They met twice a week. Destiny always arrived exactly on time, never early, never late. Leila started sitting with her back to the windows just so she wouldn't catch her own reflection looking for something in Destiny's face.

They passed notes on edits. Agreed silently on sentence structures. Polished each other's work without speaking.

It was functional.

Efficient.

Unbearable.

Leila started keeping score.

Number of group texts: 14.

Times Destiny responded to her directly: 0.

Times Leila rewrote her own sentence just to avoid sounding too much like a confession: 6.

Number of times their fingers brushed while handing off papers: 2.

Number of times Destiny flinched: 1.

She stopped keeping score after that.

Because the silence had changed.

Back in July, silence had been avoidance.

Now, it was presence. Loud and unavoidable. Like the tension before a storm, thick and humming, waiting to break.

One afternoon, after everyone else had left the study room, Destiny stayed behind to gather her things. Leila hesitated—half-standing, heart racing.

"I—" she started.

Destiny looked up.

Their eyes locked.

But then Destiny said, too quickly, "See you Thursday," and slipped out the door.

The air she left behind was full of unfinished sentences.

That night, Leila lay in bed, staring at the draft message in her Notes app again.

She didn't know why she hadn't deleted it. She hadn't looked at it in weeks. But tonight, something pulled her back.

I found your note today. The one that said 'forever friends.' I believed you. I think that's what hurts the most.

She added a new line.

Now you're here, and I still don't know what I'm allowed to say.

She locked her phone.

Buried it under her pillow.

Rolled over.

Tried not to cry.

Because it wasn't fair—how Destiny got to show up in her life again, all soft eyes and quiet glances, without ever having to explain.

It wasn't fair that her heart still jumped every time their arms brushed.

It wasn't fair that they were so close now.

And still couldn't speak.

The library was quieter than usual that night.

Rain tapped gently at the windows, and the usual hum of printers and whispering students had faded to a low murmur. It was nearly closing time, and the study room was empty—except for two people.

Leila and Destiny sat across from each other at the table, laptops open, notebooks half-filled, their group project scattered between them. Tyrese had left an hour ago, mumbling something about dinner plans and "letting the vibes settle."

Now, it was just them.

And the silence.

Not the careful, avoidant silence they'd perfected over the last two weeks. Not the fragile balancing act of side glances and subtle nods. This silence was heavier.

It was waiting.

Leila tapped her pen against her notebook, a steady rhythm. Her fingers were cold. Her heart wasn't. It pounded so loud she was sure Destiny could hear it.

Destiny hadn't looked up in a while. Her eyes were fixed on her screen, but Leila could tell she wasn't really reading.

They were both pretending.

Leila couldn't take it anymore.

She closed her notebook slowly and folded her hands in front of her.

"Destiny," she said.

The name hung in the air.

Destiny looked up, startled—like hearing her name out loud had pulled her out of a dream.

Leila's voice was low but steady. "We can't keep pretending we don't know each other."

A long pause.

Destiny blinked, then nodded. "I know."

They stared at each other, the table between them suddenly too small to contain the weight of everything left unsaid.

Leila swallowed. "I don't want to fight. But this... this is killing me."

Destiny closed her laptop with a soft click. "It's killing me too."

Leila let out a shaky breath. "Then why haven't you said anything? Why didn't you text me back? Why didn't you—" Her voice caught. "—why didn't you try?"

Destiny looked down, fingers curling into the sleeves of her sweater.

"I was scared," she said, just above a whisper. "I was scared that I'd already ruined it. That if I reached out, you'd just... hate me."

"I *did* hate you," Leila said, voice trembling. "I hated how easy it was for you to leave. How I waited for weeks—for a text, a call, *anything*—and got nothing. I hated that I couldn't stop missing you even when I tried."

Destiny flinched. "I deserve that."

Leila's hands balled into fists. "Do you have any idea what that summer was like for me? I kept telling myself I was being dramatic. That we were just friends. That I had no right to be heartbroken. But I was. I *was* heartbroken."

"I know," Destiny whispered. "Me too."

Leila stared at her. "Then why didn't you fight for me?"

"I didn't know how," Destiny said, her voice rising. "You think it was easy for me? You think I just moved on?"

"It looked like you did," Leila said. "Jayla. The stories. The silence."

"She was never you," Destiny said quickly. "Jayla was safe. She didn't ask questions. She didn't make me feel like I was standing at the edge of a cliff."

Leila blinked. "So I scared you."

"No," Destiny said. "What I felt with you scared me."

The air shifted.

Leila's voice was quiet. "Why?"

"Because it was real," Destiny said. "Because you knew me better than anyone. Because I wanted you in ways I didn't have language for at the time. And I thought... if I admitted that and you didn't feel the same, I would lose everything."

"You lost me anyway," Leila said.

Destiny nodded, tears welling in her eyes. "I know."

The rain picked up outside, a steady drumbeat against the windows.

Leila sat back in her chair. "I kept thinking... maybe I imagined it. That night on the couch. The way you held my hand. The way you looked at me."

"You didn't imagine it," Destiny said firmly. "I was falling for you. I didn't know how to handle it, and I ran. And I hate myself for that."

Silence settled again.

But it was a different silence.

One that felt like a bridge, not a wall.

Leila leaned forward. "I never stopped loving you."

Destiny's eyes widened.

"I thought I could," Leila continued. "I thought if I wrote enough, if I deleted your photos, if I let someone else sit beside me long enough... it would go away. But it didn't."

Destiny reached across the table—slow, trembling—and laid her hand on Leila's.

Their fingers didn't intertwine.

Not yet.

But they touched.

"I still love you," Destiny said. "And I'm sorry I waited this long to say it."

Leila looked down at their hands. Her voice was barely a whisper. "We're not who we were back then."

"I know," Destiny said. "But maybe that's a good thing."

They sat like that for a long time, letting the rain and the rhythm of their breath speak for them.

Finally, Destiny pulled something from her bag—a folded piece of paper, worn at the edges.

"What's that?" Leila asked.

"A letter I wrote you," Destiny said. "In July. I never sent it."

Leila took it slowly, fingers brushing Destiny's as she unfolded it.

Her eyes scanned the first few lines. Her breath caught.

She didn't speak.

She didn't have to.

When she looked up, her eyes were wet—but steady.

"Thank you," she whispered.

Destiny nodded.

They didn't fix everything that night.

But they began.

And that mattered more.

The text came late.

It was just past 11:30 p.m. when Leila's phone lit up, its soft glow cutting through the darkness of her dorm room. She was lying in bed, not quite asleep, not quite awake—floating in that half-space where thoughts feel heavier and time moves differently.

She reached for it with tired fingers.

Destiny: *Meet me. Rooftop of West Hall. Midnight.*

No emojis. No explanation.

Just a location and a time.

Leila stared at it for a few seconds, pulse already quickening. She sat up slowly, brushing her hair out of her face, feeling every beat of her heart like a second hand ticking.

There was a time she might've ignored it.

But not anymore.

She changed out of her pajamas and into a hoodie and jeans, tying her laces with more care than necessary. Her hands were shaking. She told herself it was the cold.

When she stepped outside, the air was crisp and still, the campus hushed under the weight of night. She made her way to West Hall, the tall brick building with the slanted roof and stairwell that always smelled like dust and metal.

She climbed the stairs two at a time.

When she reached the top, the heavy door creaked open to reveal the rooftop—flat, open, with a low railing and a view that stretched beyond the dorms into the dark silhouette of the city skyline.

And Destiny.

Standing near the edge, arms folded against the chill, looking like a scene from a movie Leila had seen too many times in her dreams.

Destiny turned at the sound of the door.

Their eyes met.

No one spoke.

Not yet.

Leila stepped forward slowly, her breath visible in the night air.

"You came," Destiny said, her voice quiet, almost fragile.

"You asked," Leila replied.

Destiny nodded, a half-smile tugging at her lips. "I wasn't sure if you would."

"I wasn't sure either."

They stood like that for a moment, both unsure of how to close the last bit of space between them. The wind danced around them, tugging at Destiny's braid, brushing against Leila's cheeks.

"I used to come up here a lot during orientation," Destiny said, finally breaking the silence. "It was the only place that felt quiet enough to think."

Leila glanced around. "It's beautiful."

"I wanted you to see it."

There was something in Destiny's voice—tender, hesitant, raw.

She reached into her pocket and pulled out the folded letter again. "I brought the rest."

Leila took it, carefully unfolding the second page of the note Destiny had written but never sent.

Destiny looked away as she read.

I never meant to disappear. I thought silence would hurt less than honesty. I was wrong.

You were never just a friend. You were the first person I ever saw completely—and who saw me back. That scared me. But it also saved me.

I've replayed our last night together so many times, I don't know if I remember it right anymore. But I remember how your hand felt in mine. And I remember thinking, "This could be everything."

It still could be. If you want it to.

When Leila finished, her throat felt tight.

She looked up, eyes glassy. "Why didn't you send this?"

Destiny stepped closer. "Because I didn't think I deserved to."

"You don't get to decide that," Leila said. "Not anymore."

Silence fell again—but this time, it was full of possibility.

"I meant every word," Destiny whispered. "And I meant what I said the other night, too. I still love you."

Leila's heart cracked open, all over again.

She reached out, fingers brushing Destiny's sleeve.

"Then why are we still standing this far apart?" she asked.

Destiny took the final step forward.

Their foreheads touched first, like gravity knew what they needed before they did.

And then—finally—they kissed.

It wasn't rushed.

It wasn't dramatic.

It was soft, slow, the kind of kiss that says, *I see you now. I still see you. I never stopped.*

When they pulled apart, their hands found each other without effort.

Destiny let out a breathy laugh. "You're real."

Leila smiled. "I was starting to think you were a dream."

They sat down on the edge of the rooftop, legs dangling over the side, fingers still laced.

Below them, the campus glowed with quiet windows and soft light.

"I used to imagine what this would be like," Leila admitted. "Not just being here—but being here *with you.*"

Destiny rested her head on Leila's shoulder. "What did it feel like in your imagination?"

Leila tilted her head, thoughtful. "It felt like this. Except... I didn't know it would hurt this much to get here."

Destiny nodded. "I'm sorry I made it so hard."

"You didn't make it hard," Leila said gently. "You just got lost for a while."

Destiny looked up at her. "Do you think we can... start again?"

Leila thought for a moment, then shook her head. "No."

Destiny's face fell.

But Leila reached out, tucking a strand of hair behind her ear.

"I think we can start *new*," she said. "I don't want to go back to who we were. I want to be who we are now—with everything we've learned."

Destiny smiled—really smiled.

"That sounds even better."

They stayed there for a while, watching the stars blink into view above them, listening to the hum of distant music from an open window, letting the moment settle into their bones.

No more drafts.

No more what-ifs.

No more pretending.

Just this.

Here.

Now.

The morning light felt different.

Leila woke to the sound of soft chatter in the hallway and the rustle of sheets as her roommate, Candace, got dressed across the room. Everything in the dorm looked exactly the same—same beige walls, same mini fridge humming in the corner—but something in Leila had shifted.

It wasn't the kiss, exactly.

It was the *after*.

The walking back from the rooftop side by side. The way their fingers had stayed intertwined all the way to the dorms, like letting go too soon would make it all feel like a dream again. The quiet goodnight outside her building—no more words, just a look that said *we're not pretending anymore.*

That had meant everything.

Now, as she sat up in bed, stretching her arms, Leila felt lighter.

Not like all the pain had vanished. But like it no longer defined her.

Destiny hadn't texted yet this morning. Leila didn't expect her to. That was the difference. The fear was gone. There was no game, no holding her breath waiting for a reply. There was just... space.

And the knowledge that it would be filled again. Gently.

She slipped on her shoes and grabbed her bag, tossing a granola bar into the front pocket before heading out. Her first class of the day was in East Hall—a short walk, but enough time to feel the crisp air on her cheeks and let the memory of last night anchor her.

As she crossed the quad, her phone buzzed.

Destiny: *Walking to seminar. Want to sit together?*

Leila smiled.

Yes. :)

Two letters. One punctuation mark. And suddenly, everything felt possible.

Destiny was already outside the classroom when Leila arrived, leaning against the wall, journal tucked under her arm. She wore a hoodie under her denim jacket, hair loose today. Softer.

When she looked up and saw Leila, her entire face changed.

It wasn't a dramatic smile. Just a quiet lift of the eyes. The kind of expression that says, *I'm glad it's you.*

Leila smiled back and walked toward her.

"Morning," Destiny said.

"Morning," Leila replied. "Sleep okay?"

Destiny shrugged. "Barely. Kept replaying everything. Not in a bad way, though."

Leila tucked her hair behind her ear. "Yeah. Me too."

They didn't hug. Didn't hold hands.

Not here.

Not yet.

But when they walked into class, they sat side by side.

It was small. But it mattered.

Throughout the lecture, their elbows brushed occasionally, and once, when the professor said something about "the power of narrative to rebuild what was lost," Destiny looked over and gave Leila the tiniest, knowing smile.

Leila smiled back.

Later that afternoon, Leila sat in the student center, journaling in her usual corner seat by the window. It had rained lightly while she was in class, and now the pavement outside glistened, making everything look washed clean.

She opened to a fresh page.

At the top, she wrote:

We didn't fall back into each other.

She paused.

Then added:

We found something new. Something we built after everything broke. Maybe that's even better.

Her pen moved faster now, thoughts tumbling out.

It's not perfect. We're not either. But this—this honesty—is worth more than anything we used to be.

We're not chasing the past anymore. We're choosing now. Every second.

And I think I'm okay with that.

She closed the notebook gently.

Let the words sit.

That evening, Destiny showed up outside her dorm.

No text. No warning. Just a knock.

Leila opened the door and blinked in surprise.

Destiny stood there with two paper cups of hot chocolate, both topped with way too much whipped cream.

"I didn't know if you were a whipped cream person," Destiny said. "But I kind of just... guessed."

Leila smiled. "You guessed right."

They sat on the common room couch with their drinks, legs tucked under them, laughter coming more easily now. They didn't talk about high school. Not yet. They didn't dig into every wound.

Instead, they talked about classes.

About their roommates.

About how weirdly good the campus chili fries were.

It was ordinary.

It was everything.

"I've been thinking," Destiny said after a pause, twirling the lid of her cup between her fingers.

"Uh-oh," Leila teased. "Dangerous."

Destiny grinned. "Shut up."

They both laughed.

Then Destiny turned serious.

"I know we still have a lot to work through. But I want to work through it. I want to show up this time."

Leila looked at her for a long moment.

Then nodded. "Okay."

Not a dramatic declaration.

Just... okay.

The kind of "okay" that meant yes. The kind that meant: *I hear you. I trust you. Let's try.*

They finished their drinks in silence.

When Destiny got up to leave, she hesitated by the door.

"I'll see you tomorrow?"

Leila stood too. "You'll see me."

Destiny smiled—brighter this time—and walked down the hall.

Leila closed the door gently behind her.

Then leaned against it.

She wasn't sure what they were.

Not quite a couple.

Not just friends.

But something.

Something real.

Something *new.*

And for the first time in what felt like forever, she didn't need to define it.

She just needed to live it.

ACKNOWLEDGMENTS

To my best friend, Demetri—this book wouldn't feel complete without a tribute to you. Our friendship has been one of the most meaningful constants in my life. Through the laughter, the silence, the misunderstandings, and the moments of pure joy, you've stood by me in ways that words can barely capture. There have been times when life felt messy, confusing, or overwhelming, but no matter what came our way, we always found a way back to each other. That kind of loyalty, that kind of connection—it's rare, and I don't take it for granted. You've taught me what real friendship looks like—not just when things are easy, but especially when they're not. We've had our disagreements, our distances, and even moments where it felt like we might drift apart. But somehow, we always manage to surpass the storm.

Whether it's through a conversation, a shared laugh, or simply choosing to show up for each other again and again, we prove time after time that the bond we've built is stronger than anything that tries to break it. Writing Breaking Barriers was, in many ways, a reflection of everything I've learned about growth, communication, and second chances—and much of that, I've learned with you. Our friendship helped me write this story with truth and depth, especially when exploring the emotional highs and lows between Leila and Destiny.

Thank you for unknowingly being part of the inspiration that helped shape this book's heart. You've always believed in me—even when I doubted myself—and that's a gift I'll never forget. So here's to us: to every challenge we've overcome, every lesson we've learned, and every new chapter we're still writing in our friendship. I'm beyond grateful for you, Demetri. Always.

ABOUT THE AUTHOR

La'Shayla Godfrey is a young, emerging author from Cincinnati, known for her passion for storytelling and her unique perspective. With a natural talent for capturing emotions and experiences, La'Shayla's writing reflects both her creativity and her deep connection to her roots. As a new voice in the literary world, she aims to inspire and connect with readers through powerful narratives that resonate with a wide range of audiences.

ABOUT THE PUBLISHER

The Inkwell Publishing Company is a forward-thinking literary hub dedicated to reshaping the publishing landscape. The company is driven by the belief that ideas have the power to inspire change, spark creativity, and connect humanity. At The Inkwell, authors are empowered to share their unique voices, and readers are invited into a community that values thought-provoking stories and meaningful engagement.
More than just a publisher, The Inkwell Publishing Company is a platform for innovation and collaboration. It champions new ways of thinking about literature and publishing, challenging traditional norms to create an inclusive, transformative space for creators and audiences alike. Through its commitment to quality, originality, and authenticity, The Inkwell is shaping the future of storytelling—one idea at a time.

www.ingramcontent.com/pod-product-compliance
Lightning Source LLC
Chambersburg PA
CBHW030143010826
48973CB00002B/699